The Music We're Born Remembering

by

John Leslie Butchart

FUGITIVE POETS PRESS
Greensboro, North Carolina

Published by
Fugitive Poets Press
Greensboro, NC

Copyright © 2012 John Leslie Butchart

ISBN: 978-1-938045-03-5

First Edition

Cover Photo & Design by Vince Lewis

Acknowledgments:

I want to thank B.C. Banks for helping me with research, and friends Claire Bateman, Ron Rash, Luke Whisnant, Charlotte Matthews and Ann Robinson for their insights and advice.

for Ben, Lucas & Rosie
- who never lack for wonder
or ever hesitate to share it

"Heaven is that remote music we're born remembering."

The Problem of Pain
C.S. Lewis

The Music
We're Born
Remembering

Flat on her back, Karl's fist hovering above her, knuckles white as a ball of dough, the lazy fan twirling over his head like a slow motion helicopter in a Chuck Norris flick, Claire came to a stark realization: Chuck wasn't coming to her rescue, he just wasn't coming, and nobody else, either. She'd asked for this, she'd married this, and this wasn't the first time she'd been on her back on this shag carpeting letting Karl do violence. But she didn't love him anymore and had to stop forgiving him. Getting smacked around was one thing, getting slugged in the nose, bleeding for an hour and soaking a perfectly good SuperPlush Cannon towel, well, Lord knows, that was going too far.

The Inferno

When Claire McGill turned eighteen, she partied for a weekend at Myrtle Beach with her best friend, Marla Haggerty, and paid a black-bearded tattoo artist $25 to ink a fairy on her right breast while listening to Zepplin's *Stairway to Heaven.*

"You know, some of the mummies in Egypt have tattoos," the tattooist said, the needle buzzing like a wasp trapped between his fingertips.

"Really?" Claire said. "What about the daddies?" The tattooist rolled his eyes. Claire was teetering, her brain numb, her skin throbbing. She and Marla had spent the day working on a case of beer, slathered with Panama Jack cocoa oil, baking like two chocolate chip cookies in the scorching sun and flirting with a squad of burr-headed Marines from Cherry Point.

Aloe-scented vacationers strolled the boardwalk, pausing at the tattoo shop window to watch the artists at their craft, the night sky behind them laced with pavilion lights.

Claire looked down to see her blood mixed with black ink rising in droplets from the tattoo.

Her tattooist had studied folklore at Western Carolina and explained that fairies had once been angels but were kicked out of paradise because they weren't good enough. He said the fairy would bring magic to her life but only after paying a tithe to hell.

"How does it do that?" Claire asked.

"How does it pay the tithe?" The tattooist rubbed his prickly goatee with the back of his hand and thought about it. "I don't know, maybe by doing a little evil herself."

Six years later, driving home from a dive joint named The Inferno, Claire thought about all the tithes she and her fairy had paid since that night on the boardwalk. Like a logo advertising Claire's spirit woman or girl power, the fairy was drawn in plain view where the roundness of Claire's shoulder sloped into the pectoral muscle, honey-haired with gossamer wings, no bigger than a full-grown dragonfly, but cross-eyed. The tattooist had flinched at the moment he was adding details to the tiny, pinched face.

In Samson County, below the dam that holds back Lake Haskins, the Blue River runs through the valley and under a two-lane bridge. Highway 29 takes a steep descent straight down the side of the valley, like a gigantic roller coaster that pulls the world out from under you. Local boys used the hill to generate speeds of 120 or even 140 miles per hour. At one A.M., Claire had the highway all to herself.

As she sailed down the hill, a speck of light appeared at the bottom in the center of the bridge. At first she thought it was a white cat standing in the middle of the highway. She slowed and the brakes on her piece of crap Celica squealed rebelliously, but the cat didn't stir. Then she realized that it wasn't a cat, it was a blonde-furred dog, and it just stood there. But as she reached the bottom and slowed to a stop, she saw that it was not exactly a dog either, it was a small red wolf. She stared at it through the windshield. Reflecting her headlights, the pup's eyes glowed like nuggets of gold, and its only movement was the movement of the fur covering its ribs, rising slightly with each breath. It was watching her, patiently, like it had been waiting all night for her to come down the hill and stop there. Claire thought she saw a sadness in its face, like the sadness of a lost child. She decided to get out of the car, but when she did, just as she was stepping onto the road, the wolf pup scurried into the woods. She didn't see it run, it happened at the moment she looked down to plant a foot in the road, when she stood up it had vanished. She immediately began to wonder if it had been an apparition or dream.

At senior prom, Claire had loved showing off her cheap little butt-naked fairy whose plump, perfectly rounded rump boys found strangely erotic. Drawn in shades of purple and black, the color of a fresh bruise or ripe fig, the fairy looked as crazy as Claire felt most of the time, back then before she had any responsibilities other than herself. When her mother saw it for the first time, she sighed with disgust and said it looked "slutty." More than one boy had asked if he could kiss it, and a few had.

A month after graduation, Claire was pregnant. She didn't exactly know how it had happened (they'd used a tropical-colored Trojan), but she blamed Karl, who, six years later, was waiting for her in the joyless den of their singlewide mobile home, a brand new, black, gilt-edged Bible clamped between his pale hands when she came home from The Inferno. Ever so gently, she closed the aluminum door behind her so as not to wake the boys.

"I been prayin'," Karl said from the sofa, his voice fragile and airy like someone broken and empty.

"Damn you, Karl, you scared the shit out of me. What are you doing in the dark?"

"I been prayin', prayin' real hard," he said.

"Well, good for you."

"It is good for me, and for you and the boys." In the surrounding forest, the hollow abdomens of hundreds of male cicadas were vibrating, making the singlewide hum like a hydroelectric dam. "Sweetie, I miss holdin' you so freakin' much," Karl moaned.

"You try to jump me, I'll puke on you," Claire said.

"I don't care," he muttered plaintively. Claire hated hearing him whine. She wanted to kick him in the face and pressed her right foot into the soiled shag carpeting to thwart the impulse.

"Baby, I gotta tell you something. Honestly, I never felt this way before. God's come into me and tore me up, made me all emotional. I keep wanting to set things right by you and the boys, I swear that's become my heart's desire."

"Don't worry about it, Karl," Claire said.

"What do you mean, 'don't worry?'"

"I've decided to leave you."

"You what? For real?"

"Yep. For as real as I can make it."

After more groaning and whining, Karl finally manned up and went to bed without her.

She sat on the concrete slab they called a patio. The sky had cleared, but the atmosphere was tepid at two A.M., raising sweat, it was August, and Pabst seeped from her

4

pores. She draped her red banner of hair over the back of the lawn chair and looked at the sky, smoked a menthol Marlboro, each inhalation tingling and burning her tonsils. She thought about Karl and their boys, Toby and Sam, and how her life was like a constellation of stars, kind of a big, empty dipper: seeing double, try as she might, she couldn't get the stars into focus.

In high school, all she'd wanted was to play lacrosse and maybe coach some day. Slight of frame but fast as a skink, she was the highest scorer in the history of Newton Grove. She flexed her arms and pecs, in the moon's blue glow her fairy shimmered under a sheen of sweat. A breeze swept across the distant treetops, a moment later reaching her, chilling her skin, and she thought about going to find her letter jacket decorated with tiny brass lacrosse sticks, then remembered she had folded it up and packed it away in a plastic box in her parents' attic. She fell asleep, the cigarette between her fingers forming a worm of ash until a breeze scattered it across the silvery grass as her brain ran away on its own and attempted to fabricate a dream.

Around 7 A.M. she heard knocking. When she opened her eyes, Toby was watching her through the sliding glass door. He was her oldest, age six, and his mullet needed trimming. He probably wondered why mommy was sleeping on the patio. He held up an empty milk jug. "We're out," he mouthed.

She went inside. Sam, her youngest at four years, was watching cartoons, equally absorbed in picking his nose. She left without speaking to Karl and headed over to the Scotsman for a pack of cigarettes and quart of milk.

5

There was a time when Claire had enjoyed being married. And she loved her boys but wished one of them had been a girl. Maybe a daughter she could play Barbies with would make life more fulfilling. Her father had built her a two-story pink house when she was four, and every Christmas she'd gotten more Barbies and outfits. Her mother had even stuck a Barbie and Ken on her wedding cake, which was a store-bought sheet cake from Food Lion and needed a centerpiece. At sixteen, with her clothes off, Claire thought she looked a lot like Barbie, lithe and rosy, almost perfect.

Sheila was working the register at the Scotsman. During the night somebody had tried to break in but only got as far as busting out the lower panel on the front door. Minuscule glass bits flickered in the morning sunlight.

"Who do you think did it?" Claire asked standing at the checkout counter trying not to stare at the black hair curling from the mole on Sheila's cheek.

"Some meth head, probably," Sheila said. "Sheriff Clancy came by and drank three cups of coffee while he looked at the door and talked to Henry. He said it was the second time in a month somebody broke into a place or tried to." Sheila took Claire's payment. "Could be a car come by or something and scared him off before he could complete the job." She dropped a few coins into Claire's palm. "The Sheriff said Karl has become a Christian."

"Um-hm. We'll see if it sticks. Wonder how the Sheriff knew about it."

"He goes to Nu Life," Sheila said. Sheila was only seventeen but had the vacant expression, I-don't-give-a-shit attitude, satanic tats, and biker tramp makeup you often see on country girls. "I visited once or twice but them folks are too fuckin' loud for me. They got a full-scale rock band and a big-ass speaker system like something at a Widespread concert." Sheila handed Claire a warm sausage biscuit snuggly wrapped in grease-soaked wax paper.

"What's that?" Claire asked. "Charity?"

"Do you want it?"

"Did I ask for it?"

"No, but do you want it?" Sheila asked. "I gotta git rid of 'em, it's after ten. Take some home to the boys and Karl why don'tcha."

"Sure, Sheila. Thanks." Sheila put four biscuits into a paper sack. "Hey Sheila, over at Nu-Life, who's in charge there now, you know, who's the pastor? I heard they got somebody new from Winston-Salem."

"I forget his name but he's a nice fella," Sheila said. "He comes in here sometimes. I seen him peeking at a Penthouse, so he ain't all that righteous. He's got a nice smile though. Pretty teeth. Good hair. He buys a lot of TicTacs, like the multipacs, you know ..."

"Oh cool," Claire said to cut her off, because Sheila could gab like a goose. "See ya later, Sheila. Thanks for the biscuits."

Later that morning, things got worse. Karl started shaming her with his holier-than-thou work ethic.

"Seen my camo Chucks?" he yelled from the bedroom. "Never mind. Found 'em!" He walked down the hallway and entered the kitchen. Claire was thumbing through a story about Brad and Angelina in a *People* magazine her mother had loaned her. "I found 'em stuck under the bed." He sat on a kitchen stool, wedged his bare feet into the ratty old Converse.

"You don't want to talk about it, do you?" he asked, watching her flip pages. "You don't want to talk about what Jesus has done for me." She didn't look up. "Well, in due time," he said, and without another word he went outside to mow the lawn.

She almost felt grief for the dead Karl. At least when he was high, his idiot ways were understandable. She watched him through the kitchen window. He was pushing the Craftsman to the center of the backyard. The grass was as high as a young wheat field and along the path Karl pushed their old piece of crap mower the blades of grass bowed over like hair smoothed down by a barber's hand. She usually did the mowing, while Karl watched from the patio, a Rolling Rock dangling from thumb and forefinger.

In his floppy shoes and baggy old gym shorts it was terribly obvious she'd married a clown. His curly brown hair bounced as he walked, he didn't have an ass, his skinny legs were as white as the underbelly of a county fair piglet. But his body had never been the magnet, no, it was that smirky smile and gleam in his eyes, the devilish look that said, "Yeah, I know, life sucks, let's get drunk and screw." Now, other than pity, she didn't know what to feel for him. Where had her love gone? Their marriage was as stagnant as the algae water in the half-inflated baby pool he was dragging across the yard.

This God thing had come too high and hard, like the

throw home that split Jimbo Newsome's skull open in the softball game last September, and he still wasn't thinking straight. Karl had changed overnight, something had gotten into him, something called the Holy Ghost, and his desire to drink had vanished. That desire, that thirst, that demon, had taken them both right to the brink. Claire had asked herself many times why she'd even married him. She'd just wanted to have a life, but not exactly this life.

After mowing the lawn, Karl scraped the trailer. Paint had flaked off the aluminum in places and orange rust streaks had followed that made the singlewide look like an old urinal. Karl used a wire brush to attack the problem. Claire was fairly amazed.

"By the grace of God, I am a new man," he announced coming in the door that incredible evening two weeks earlier, after falling to his knees at the top of Boykin Dam and asking Jesus into his heart. In the back part of her mind she had stored a thought, tucked it away like a jar of Gram's spiced peaches waiting for the holidays: maybe Karl had gone to the dam to jump, to end it all, an easy escape from his addiction to alcohol and guilt for being a slack-ass husband, but then he'd heard a voice, maybe the very voice of God, or Jesus had appeared from the clouds, she had no inkling exactly what had happened, but it was something miraculous, it had to be, and what so disturbed her was the possibility that he had gotten to the edge of that cement cliff and that her bitching had pushed him there, her and those once-a-day pints of Jim Beam, so now the notion crossed her mind – or was it a wish? – maybe he should have gone ahead and jumped. Planning a funeral would be easier than living with a born again man.

Claire's mother, Joyce ("my friends call me J.J."), was becoming exceedingly lumpy all over, so lumpy that Claire was embarrassed going out in public with her on their routine Sunday excursion.

As they stood in line at Biscuit Hut, a woman behind a glass window was making scratch biscuits, rolling them out, cutting rounds and flinging them expertly into a dented baking tray, and Claire noticed that her mother's skin had the color and texture of biscuit dough. She was afraid her mother was turning into a human biscuit.

"Momma, you eat too many biscuits," Claire said when they had settled in at a table with their biscuits and coffees.

"If we can't have our simple pleasures this life would not be worth the frustration," J.J. said, sounding serious, like this was her philosophical summation of the meaning of life.

"Hopefully there is more to life than biscuits and Big Lots," Claire said. Her mother raised a fluffy biscuit to her mouth, egg and country ham drooping out its edges, took a big bite, and winked at her petite daughter. "Momma, there is more to life, at least I hope there is. Karl is getting along with God now and excited about being born again, but I don't know about all that, I really don't."

"I don't know about all that either, sweetie. Seems to me if God is love then that's just about the long and short of it, and everything else is pure hoopla. You know, churches want your money, seems to me that's why they have to put on such a show. At least that's been my observation."

"If a piece of that country ham stuck in your throat and you choked to death right here and now would you go to heaven? That's the question."

"That's the question? Hmmm, maybe I would and maybe I wouldn't, that'd be something for God to decide."

"Right, I think that's how it works. So aren't you the least little bit curious about what comes next after this life?"

"No, not really."

"See, that's what I mean. Your surface existence has rubbed off on me and now my husband is born again and I've got to decide what to do. Should I keep him or should I cut him lose."

"Cut your loses, sweetie, Karl will never be good husband material, with or without God."

"Momma, you are a hard, hard woman to be so overweight."

J.J. found that hilarious and almost choked on her biscuit just as Claire had forewarned.

"See, you're choking now, for being so mean," Claire said.

J.J. cleared her throat, sipped her coffee, composed herself.

"I think what you're talking about is your own crisis point," J.J. said.

"What is that?"

"A crisis point is when you see plainly that you must make a decision of some importance, as in a life-changing decision."

"How come you never talked to me like this before? About *crisis points.*"

"I guess the time has just come."

"So are you gonna help me decide what I should do?"

"Claire, you have always been smart and pretty and pig-headed, but you've never known what to do with yourself and your talents. And sweetie, I have never known how to advise you, because, you see, I am stuck in a similar, rather dead-end rut of a life. Now, I have just accepted my fate, and my cholesterol level, and my TV-addicted husband, but this is my life, the life God seems to have given me or at least wants me to have, so I'm going to live it the best I know how, and I suggest you try to do the same."

"You want me to settle for my life as it is now?" Claire asked, her face displaying the deep, inner angst behind her question.

"Claire, do you really have a choice?" J.J. said. "I mean, if you think church can improve your life, by all means give it a try. What's it going to hurt, sweetie, I mean, really, what's it going to hurt?"

After biscuits, Claire drove her mother to Big Lots to search for Japanese lanterns and yard gnomes. Her mother liked exotic things from the Orient most of all. She called it "the elegant simplicity of the Asian aesthetic." She'd attended Sampson Community College at the age of 45 to take art classes, and now she used the elegant simplicity of the Asian aesthetic to counteract her husband's wall-to-wall enchantment with NASCAR. On every square inch of their den he'd hung posters and shelves of replica cars and souvenir beer mugs, and half a bumper from Sterling Marlin's Ford Thunderbird that crashed at the Valleydale

Meats 500 in 1991, and all kinds of other racing crap, until J.J. insisted on a sunroom for herself, which he gladly built using leftover lumber from his brother Alsroe's housing development in Clinton.

The checkout lady at Big Lots was a "nice Negro woman" – that's what J.J. called them – who, for no apparent reason, gave her an extra ten percent off on top of the already enormously discounted prices. J.J. gushed with gratitude.

"It was just ten percent," Claire said on the way to the car. "Good gosh Momma. You'd have thought she donated a lung to you."

"I know. But it was just so nice of her. So many of them hold a grudge against us, from the Jim Crow days, but not her. I liked her." Which goes to prove, Claire thought, that for many Southerners racism has a sensitive side.

"She was very nice," Claire agreed. Ever since Big Lots had opened its doors in Newton Grove, her mother had been a regular, but this was icing on the cake. After this, she would be a Big Lots VIP Shopper until the day she died.

Big Eddie was home when they drove up and he came into the summer heat on the carport to make sure he got a hug from his precious peanut. His familiar Old Spice smell made Claire feel two again.

"Daddy," Claire cooed, turning her face into the warmth of his T-shirt-encased chest. His name was Big Eddie but he was only 5' 8" and thick with both muscle and a lifetime of Budweiser.

"Hey pigeon, where'd ya'll get off to? Big Lots?"

"Um-hm, Momma found a gnome spitter. And we found you a Dale Earnhardt thingamabob," Claire said.

"A wall plaque," J.J. clarified.

"Yeah, a wall plaque," Claire said, wresting it out of the plastic bag.

"That's real nice," her father said, squinting at it. "What the hell's a gnome spitter?"

"It's a thing that spits water," Claire said, "like you see in a pond."

"We don't have a pond," Big Eddie said, "oh god, am I gonna have to dig you a pond now?" he groaned, wiping his face with a meaty hand. "Let's get some tea. I just submerged from my nap."

They sat at the dinette with tall green glasses of sweet iced tea.

"The sun has sucked out all my energy like a big fat tick," J.J. said using her unusual talent for imagery.

"How's the kids?" her father asked.

"Toby's burned place is healing up real good," Claire said. "Karl took them to church this morning."

"So, what's this I heard about Karl?" he asked. She could hear a snarl in his question.

"He's changed, Daddy, I swear, it's like a miracle or something. I was telling Momma, he's quit drinking, and yesterday he was up early mowing the grass and scraping the trailer." Claire's eyes lit up over the rim of her raised tea. She gulped and sighed, feeling cooler. "He was out in the scorching sun flecked all over with rust specks, sweating like a hog in season, and he hates to sweat. I swear, I think he's found God for real."

"Sounds like," her father said doubtfully. He hated Karl so much he daydreamed about killing him and often admitted his imagined schemes to Claire. The first time Karl slapped her and split her lip, she went straight to her daddy And her daddy went straight for his shotgun.

"Daddy, you cannot, you must not, shoot Karl!" Claire had pleaded.

"Why can't I? Give me one good reason or I'm gonna blow his dangfool balls off!"

"You want the children to see their grandpa being a murderer? Going to prison? Do you? You love them too much to let that happen, I know you do." She'd gripped the cold barrels of the 12 gauge, yet somehow the violence in his voice comforted her, made her feel loved and childlike again. Clutching the steel barrels it dawned on her how death can be so quickly delivered, and she'd taken the heavy old gun away from him and put it back in the bedroom closet.

Anyhow, by the time her father would've gotten to the trailer, Karl would've been passed out on the sofa. In the morning, he wouldn't remember the fight, might not remember hitting her. A busted lip was no reason for her father to kill him. She'd gotten a lot of busted lips playing lacrosse. Her tolerance for pain was a gift, maybe it was something from Big Eddie's side. His great grandfather had immigrated from Ireland during the potato famine and opened the first granite quarry in Virginia. McGill ambition put her husband to shame. It was bad enough Karl couldn't hold a job, but beating her up, well, that was low life behavior, and low life was what he came from. His father had even done a turn in Central Prison for auto theft, and his mother had worked as a barmaid up until she died of lung cancer breathing other people's miseries at Brightside Tavern. By contrast, Big Eddie had run his own Gulf service station and done some banging around on the late model circuit. And J.J., she'd gotten training in the Asian aesthetic, had cooked most of Paula Deen's heart attack recipes, and had even directed a few weddings at Magnolia Street Baptist Church.

After that shotgun scare, Claire stopped telling her father about Karl's assaults. Her bruises weren't bad enough to put Karl in the grave and her father in the penitentiary. She could take just about anything. She just had to keep her mouth shut. She could do that. Stubbornness was another McGill trait.

Jasmine

"Goin' to church with me tonight?" Karl asked at dinner. Toby watched her for the answer.

"What about the boys?" Claire asked.

"I want them to go, too. They have a terrific youth group. I want my family to come to Jesus as a whole unit."

"Youth groups aren't for kids their size."

"Well they got something for their size."

"I don't have anything to wear," Claire lied.

"Casual is okay. Lots of people wear jeans, even shorts. It's come-as-you-are."

"I don't have anything nice," Claire said. "You go on without me."

"I'm gonna take the boys with me."

"That would be splendid, Karl. Real splendid."

As soon as Karl left, she slipped into fresh jeans and a lime green spaghetti strap top, pulled her buoyant red locks into a ponytail, and headed over to Marla's. When she pulled up in front of Marla's bungalow in her rings-shot-smoke-spewing '78 Celica, her very best friend was on the back porch, where she had set up the TV to watch *American Idol*. Marla had strung the porch railing in tiny twinkling lights. She even had a plastic palm tree outlined in green and pink lightrope. She'd made a pitcher of sangria and was frying hamburger for tacos.

"Who you expecting? Tommy?"

17

"He said he would drop by after his shift," Marla said. She was showing off her tanned shoulders in a blue sundress and had put some curls in her blonde hair. "Karl still saved?"

"Looks that way." Claire twisted the cap off a Corona. "He's been doing all kinds of work around the house."

"You know what the problem with you is?"

"No, tell me."

"You are way too gullible when it comes to him."

"I know. I know. *I know.*"

"You should've left him after Toby was born. You've let him trample on your self-image. When somebody does that day after day, pretty soon your own true self is eroded away, like mud in a storm."

"He's eroded me, huh."

"Right, that's what he's done. You should've left him a long, long time ago."

"You already said that." Claire stretched out on a lounge chair, the springy fold up kind you carry to the beach. "I get it, Marla. That seems to be the general opinion about my husband."

Marla had a book on spouse abuse entitled *Beat It! Surviving Spouse Abuse,* and she liked to quote from it. That had to be where the self-image insight came from.

Marla rolled on, "But of course you couldn't face it because you will not and cannot admit failure. So, you are in denial. *Total* denial. You can't admit it to anybody. Not even to me. Oh shit ..." Marla sprang off the porch railing to check on the hamburger.

"Burned it, didn't you," Claire yelled through the open

French doors.

"Just barely!"

Claire watched the American idols singing together onstage under a barrage of lights and wondered why Marla had the sound turned down. Did every small town kid dream of something like this? Making a million dollars on *American Idol* or *Survivor*? Why had she never dreamed of anything like that? Marla was a good example of a small town survivor. She had turned her patio into a tropical island with a twenty dollar palm tree from Walmart. Of course, Marla did everything with her own flair and enthusiasm. She had bought the house all by herself on a nurse's salary, cleaned it up, painted the rooms in colors from Lowe's Designer Selections, pulled up the carpeting and restored the oak floors. There weren't many women in their twenties who could do that.

Marla returned licking the fingers of one hand and holding out a cracker with a slice of Cracker Barrel on it, which she gently shoved into Claire's open mouth like it was a rehearsed feeding habit.

"I love Chris Daughtry," Marla said, glancing at the TV. "Now that's a man for ya. And he's a Carolina boy."

"He's too short for me," Claire said.

"All the big stars are shorties," Marla reminded her. "Like Tom Cruise, he's practically a midget."

"He's one of those scientists or whatever."

"I think you mean Scientology," Marla said. "Now there's a fucked up religion. You know, I was thinking, it's good that Karl found God when he did, otherwise he'd've had the snot beat out of him." She was referring to their plan for the next time Karl beat her up. Claire and the boys would move in with Marla, then they'd call Jeb, Claire's brother. Jeb was buddies with a Deputy Sheriff named Howie. Howie had gone to high school with Claire and still carried a crush on her, and he had already promised them that if Karl raised blood again, he would have some raised in return. Under "shield of law" was how Howie had put it.

If your husband likes to beat you, it's good to have a nurse for your best friend. One time when Karl smashed her nose, Claire had run to Marla's house and Marla had packed her face in ice. That's when Marla devised the *Howie Plan.* She remembered the anger flashing in Marla's eyes and how pleased she was discussing revenge.

Marla was smart. She'd gone to Sampson Community College to get her RPN and taken a job at Sampson Memorial Hospital. Anything you needed to know about broken bones, birthing, heart attacks, car accidents, horrific farm injuries, and, of course, alcohol poisoning, drug overdoses and spouse abuse, Marla had experienced first-hand.

"How's my little dreamboat?" Marla asked. She'd been worried about Sam ever since he burned his arm on a hotplate at Jeb's. Claire had shown up on her doorstep with Sam screaming and Marla had doctored him. She'd gently washed off the Crisco Claire had slathered on the burn and replaced it with a special ointment she just happened by the grace of God to have in the house. Otherwise an emergency room visit would have cost them a fortune.

"He's fine," Claire said. "God I love my little fellas."

20

"Too bad Karl came with the deal, huh."

"Yeah. But I'm glad I kept them."

When Claire had learned that she was pregnant with Toby, Marla was the first to hear about it, even before J.J. or Karl. After the doctor broke the news, Claire had just wanted to get high; the weight of reality, heavy as it was, maybe the zygote in her uterus would simply disappear if she got high enough. She and Marla had driven out to the dam around dusk when the sun melting into Lake Haskings made it look like a sheet of hammered gold. They'd found an old rusted crank wheel as tall as they were and climbed on it like it was a Jungle Gym and tried to turn it. When it budged with a sharp, frightening squeak they laughed and looked for something to happen: the water was still gushing from the two spillways at the base of the two hundred foot dam, and for a while whatever the downstream of their lives held in store for them was about as distant as the bright blue and yellow rafts, the size of Fruit Loops, at Blue River Tubing in the shadowy gape of the valley below.

Claire helped Marla cut up onions and tomatoes to go on the tacos.

"I hope you realize this religious conversion of his could well be a short-term phenomenon," Marla said.

"I suppose."

"You *suppose?*"

"That's what I said."

"But you don't love him, Claire."

"I know."

"That's a fact you are going to have to eventually embrace," Marla said.

"They did it," Tommy said, walking in, a pink sheet of paper in his hand. "They fuckin' done did it. They're shutting down Crescent. You know that company in India bought it, and now they are shutting it the fuck down and moving all the looms to some place called Chennai. Everybody knew it was comin' and just bent over with a smile on their faces. All three hundred and seven of us. Hell, what are some of them old folks gonna to do? All they know is the mill. At least I got other skills. Hell, I'm only twenty-five. I wasn't gonna be there forever anyway."

"That's probably what some of those people said thirty years ago," Marla said, handing him a Corona wifely-like even though they'd been dating less than a month.

"Yeah, probably," Tommy said. "Now I'm free n' clear to branch out and try something new. They gave us two weeks of get lost pay. Is that tacos?"

"That's what it is," Marla said.

"Hi, Claire," Tommy said, noticing her on the sofa.

Tommy Holt wasn't a real stud of a guy and normally you couldn't pry an entire sentence out of his mouth, but he was cute with blonde curls and round cheeks and Claire had always tolerated him. Marla said he was the best lover she'd ever had, except for the way his beer gut made him look pregnant. With lovemaking skills going for him, he didn't need verbal skills, but tonight he was talking a blue streak. He'd taken a shower and smelled like Brut.

"Hell, who wants to spend their life making women's crew socks," he muttered during their Mexican meal.

"You've got bigger fish to fry, Tommy," Marla said, her voice spiced with encouragement.

"I know," Tommy said, crunching into his fifth taco. "I know I do."

"What are those other skills you were talking about?" Claire asked. Tommy thought for a moment.

"Hunting. That's one skill," he said. "Rifle or bow, don't matter."

Claire had known him in high school. He was a guard and during the summer they'd gone running together a few times to get in shape for the start of the season, football for him, lacrosse for her.

"Sheetrock. I know plaster. And painting, interior and exterior, trim, whatever it takes," Tommy said. She remembered how long his stride was, how grown up he seemed for a junior. He'd asked her out once but she was preoccupied, and plus she was a sophomore and felt like such a kid. She was still a virgin then.

"Football, of course," he added.

"You can write," Claire said.

"I can?"

"Remember that poem you read in Miss Lassiter's class?"

"I almost forgot about that," he said. He seemed to be growing more somber as his new situation sank in.

They decided to drink sangria and smoke some weed. Tommy watched Discovery Channel while they cleaned up, something about pythons and how they can eat anything, even whole monkeys.

It was ten o'clock when they drove out to The Inferno, the cinderblock juke joint off Highway 29, mostly for locals since it was a half-mile from the blacktop, down a gravel road that cut through a stretch of Loblolly Pines then alongside the Snyder's soybean fields where the sparks of thousands of lightning bugs danced in the darkness.

The patch of land occupied by The Inferno was also owned by the Snyders. One of the sons, Lewis, had been running the place since he graduated from high school. The other Snyder children had gone off to college or married and gotten away.

Most everybody ran off from Newton Grove if they got half a chance, so the local scene was populated with people who knew each other way too well. Friends since birth, high school teammates and sweethearts, as well as mortal enemies, all thrown together by their mistakes and ignorance, all surrendered to the listless textile town way of life and its shrunken opportunities, stuck in the sandhills of North Carolina without enough sense to turn toward the fertile piedmont crescent or wistful Blue Ridge Mountains, like wayward pioneers lost on the trail, who probably never had a compass to begin with.

There were six shiny choppers lined up in front of The Inferno. Tommy paid for a pitcher and Claire dropped a handful of quarters in the jukebox and started dancing. She danced with some of the bikers, danced with Marla, danced by herself – it was late and she hadn't called Karl, and she didn't care – she wanted to forget him. She had her eye on a tall, ruddy-skinned man with long black hair who was sitting by himself at the bar. She didn't have the nerve to go over and flirt outright but she tried to dance as seductively as she could in the middle of the beer-moist cement floor. He looked like an Indian. The Croatan had never been given a reservation in Sampson County but there were a lot of them around. He could have been a migrant, topping tobacco or pulling corn, peaches wouldn't be ripe until August, but the man wasn't Mexican, definitely more Indian-looking. Claire didn't know why he interested her, except that he was damn good-looking. She hadn't been with a man other than Karl since high school when she slept with her first real boyfriend, Steve Autry. Nobody was talking to the Indian, he seemed to be alone, but nobody minded him being there.

A high degree of cross-pollination made the population of Sampson County more original-looking than anywhere else in America, and many of the genetic blends were beautiful people – mocha skin, blue eyes, black hair, or blond hair and brown eyes, skin the color of goldenrod – a milkshake of races.

A strange rumor had to do with Irish monks who were said to have settled in Sampson County in 700 A.D. and bred with the local Indians. There were actually some Croatans who had red hair. It was probably just a legend, but, since Claire was Irish, it was something she was curious about. All through school, she'd been called "Red" and "Carrot Top." Her mother and father had made her proud of her Irish heritage, but it was still humiliating when she was small. Maybe that was also something that had made her tough, that had given her a thick skin. The life of a redhead was nothing you'd wish on anyone.

She wondered if she got pregnant by the Indian sitting alone at the bar if their baby would have red hair, like a McGill. If he asked her name, she would say, "Claire

McGill," not "Claire Craddock." She hated the name Craddock even though Karl's second cousin was Bobby Crash Craddock, the country singer, and Bobby Crash had given them two crystal candlesticks as a wedding gift. She had set them on top of the entertainment center they scored at Big Lots for a song and she had put gold candles in them that never stood up straight, so she had just as soon Bobby Crash had never sent them, since it was the only crystal anything they owned.

Tommy was playing pool with Johnny Coble (people called him *Johnny C*), their pot connection. Tommy and Johnny C had gone out back and smoked some, both were blotto, Johnny C had a huge stupid grin on his face.

The bikers cranked their choppers all at once and the deafening explosions of those big two-piston engines vibrated the cinderblock walls, rattling the neon Miller beer sign and bottles of beer stacked in the cooler. Johnny C pretended an earthquake had hit, stumbling back and forth trying to keep his balance.

"You wanna shoot some with us Little Red?" Johnny C asked.

"No thank you," Claire said. "I need a toke. You holdin' some?"

"Now that's a stupid question if I ever heard one," Tommy said. "It's some good shit Johnny C come up with."

"Locally grown produce is always the best," Johnny C said, palming her a fat joint.

She went out back and lit up, burning through half the joint in three monster inhalations. Johnny C's stash was sensimilia, the female flower, the most potent part of the plant. Claire felt herself being lifted off the planet for a minute or two. The next thing she knew she was having an out-of-body experience: she was watching a barred owl in a tall pine tree, and the owl was watching The Inferno. Mice were coming out of The Inferno. At first she thought they were leaving for the night, but then she noticed they were going to the dumpster, a string of perfect white mice in a perfect line, like pearls on a necklace, or tiny chorus girls dressed in white mink coats; and she was thrilled with the idea that the owl was going to swoop down on one and snatch it away, but it never did. The owl just watched them without curiosity, as if standing guard in the night, the mice oblivious to its presence. She didn't know how much time had passed before she realized she was thirsty. She went inside, the air conditioning immediately drying the sweat on her skin. She felt her nipples stiffen. She got a frosty beer from Angie, who was tending bar. Angie was a local potter known for her azure glazes. She dated Lewis and tended bar whenever he needed her help.

The Indian got up and left without so much as blowing Claire a kiss. She hurried to the door to see what kind of car he drove. It was a 1972 Camaro, restored, with green metallic paint and airbrushed flames, the same model she'd lost her flower to Steve Autry in. What a small world it was, a county-size world.

It dawned on Claire that The Inferno's customers, after the departure of the Indian, were all kids who'd been left behind, kids for whom a college experience in Chapel Hill or Raleigh or Greensboro was just not in the cards. Kids who had settled for swimming in the rock quarry and working at Walmart, the community college, or the visitor's center at the Civil War battleground.

Marla was reading a book and chewing on the plastic filter of a Doral between puffs.

"What are you reading?" Claire asked, slipping into the booth across from her. She could read the title herself, *'The English Patient.'*

"I never saw that," Claire said.

"I did, but the book's a whole lot better." Marla lowered the paperback, looked at Claire.

"You are really fucked up aren't you?"

"Um ... yeah."

"Did you sign up for college yet?"

"No."

"And why not?"

"Because we don't have any money."

"You can get a loan."

"I don't want a loan."

"Darlin', are you gonna let this town get the best of you? If you don't get some more education, you will not have a fighting chance at a real life." Marla was such a frickin' know it all.

"Why do you do this to me?"

"You hear me? *Claire?*"

"I hear you."

"I'm going to take you down there myself if you don't get off your ass and go. Hell, I'll loan you the money."

"Okay, okay," Claire said. "I gotta pee."

Tommy grabbed her when she came out of the bathroom. They were in the narrow hallway where no one could see them. He held her by the waist and pulled her so close she could feel the roundness of his beer gut.

"Let go of me before Marla comes around that corner," Claire said.

"How come you and me never got together?" He slurred his words.

"'Cause I got hitched to Karl, I guess."

"We could mess around," he said. "Secret-like."

"Shut your damn mouth, Tommy. Marla is only my best friend ever. I'm not going betray her. You sure as hell ain't worth it." She pushed him away. "You're trouble when you're drunk, Tommy, you always were, even in high school. You don't have the nerve to come on to me unless you're drunk, how sad is that."

Karl knocked on Marla's door about 8:30 A.M. Claire had passed out on the sofa, never called home, Marla and Tommy were back in the bedroom.

"Nobody ever comes to this door," Claire said after opening the front door enough to see out with one eye.

"Why didn't you come home?" Karl asked. "You get drunk again? Dumb question, I know, you look like shit. I was worried, and the boys was worried. This fuckin' shit's gotta stop, Claire."

"How many times've you done the same to me? Huh? How many times? I don't have enough fingers and toes to count with."

"What is wrong with you? Why are you doing this? You are gonna have to give me a second chance, Claire."

"Why? Damnitall Karl, *why?*"

"Okay, look. Let's not argue about it right now. I need for you to come home and watch the boys. I need you there by noon."

"Why's that?"

"Because I've got a job interview at one."

"Where?"

"Walmart."

"Oh great."

"They got benefits. We need some benefits. Will you come home?"

"Yeah, sure. I'll be there."

"Thanks baby," Karl said, stepping off the front stoop. "Thanks a lot. We're gonna work it out baby, I'm telling you, we are gonna work it out."

Karl insisted on everybody going to Applebees in Clinton to celebrate him getting the job at Walmart. Claire's parents met them there. They were cordial to Karl but eyed him like a rabid dog. The dog you used to like but now were afraid to pet.

"Walmart's the biggest company in the world in terms of retail chains," Karl said. The boys listened to every word – Karl had told them about the fifteen percent employee discount they could use in the toy department. Claire had mentioned the discount to J.J., who was also listening closely. "It's got over twenty-five hundred stores so that's how they can give such good prices. It's called *buying power*."

"I heard it was Walmart that shut down Edmonds Drugstore. They couldn't compete with that *buying power*,"

Big Eddie said.

"Yeah but, Big Eddie, is it not better for folks to have low prices on their medicine, folks who need it and don't have much money and have to eat dog food, like old people do? And also Walmart employs about a dozen people in the pharmacy and cosmetics and health products sections of the store, so that's about twice as many people with jobs, twice as many good, reliable taxpayers. So then the county's got money for roads and parks, and for putting a new pier on the lake, so you can go fishing in comfort. The pier on Lake Haskings was donated by Walmart. I didn't know that until I went to orientation."

"I'm not so convinced about the wonderfulness of Walmart," Big Eddie said. He hadn't taken the trouble to shave and his beard looked like a coating of golden sand on his cheeks. "They don't give us that *orientation*, but it seems like everybody I know has a relative who works there now, and I'm afraid the Walmarting of America is going to have some kind of fallout one day." Big Eddie raised his menu to shield himself.

"What's the procedure for taking advantage of your extra discount?" J.J. asked.

"You have to be a spouse, if you're not the person under Walmart employment his or herself. So you'd have to let Claire get it for you," Karl explained.

"We go shopping all the time together anyway Momma," Claire said.

"Big Eddie, if you want, we can check out the fishing and hunting section, and I can get you the discount," Karl said. Big Eddie lowered his menu.

"I would appreciate that, Karl, I've been lookin' to rethink my tackle."

"They got some nice johnboats you can catalog order. Maybe you and me could go in on one." The brightness of Karl's idea shone across the table and made the boys smile.

"Maybe so," Big Eddie said. "Maybe so. We'll see."

That night Karl was still being gentle and sweet. They had sex. It was better than usual owing to Karl's sobriety and him giving more attention to foreplay and making sure he was pleasing her. After, Claire went outside to smoke. It was another balmy summer night. She heard dogs barking in the distance back and forth, having some sort of dog conversation, and she began to wonder if she and Karl might make it after all − after all the times he hit her that she never told anybody about, and after all the horrible things she had said to him − things that cut deep into what little confidence he had, words that broke the bones of his being. She eased into bed and lay there studying his face in the moonlight. He wasn't that bad-looking. He was smarter than he gave himself credit for. He'd probably be a good Walmart employee. He knew tires and lube pretty good and that's where they'd assigned him.

On the following Saturday, Claire went to visit her grandmother, Edna Rose McGill. The nursing home was about a two-hour drive down Highway 29 toward Greensboro. Karl stayed behind to watch the boys, and said he might try to track down his father that afternoon. His father worked at a textile mill in Harrells, near Rockingham.

"Hi Grams," Claire said. Her grandmother didn't stir. She lay in bed in a room that reeked of urine. The nursing home normally did a good job keeping the residents comfortable but her Grams had wet her bed and the dampness had made her cold. Claire went to the bathroom and filled a plastic basin with warm water. She pulled back the sheets and pulled Grams to a sitting position. Her house dress was wet all over one side. She lifted it over her head. Grams' skin was thin and wrinkled like rumpled cellophane. Claire gave her a warm wipe-down bath. She'd done it a hundred times before when Grams was living at her parents' house. She was a teenager then and the task was more distasteful, but she'd gotten used to it and went about the job like a well-trained nurse.

When Grams was clean and dry, Claire rubbed on a lavender smelling lotion and dusted her crotch and fanny with talcum powder. Claire noticed Grams reacting to the smell of the lotion. She looked at Claire deliberately but without a glimmer of recognition. Claire dropped a clean, baby blue nightgown over her head, then lifted her into a wheelchair.

She stripped off the urine-stained sheets, wiped down the plastic protective cover with a disinfectant soap and water mixture, and remade the bed with fresh linens.

She pushed her Grams to the sunroom. It was raining. The sunroom was quiet. For an hour, Claire sat with her, holding her hand, watching rivulets of rainwater course down the window panes.

She took Grams back to her room and lifted her into bed. She was as light as a bird, as if her bones had become hollow. Beside Grams' bed, on a nightstand shelf, there was a Bible, the one Grams had carried to church every Sunday. Claire slid it from its place alongside other books that Grams would never read again. The pages fell open to Psalms. A jasmine flower had been placed there, at Psalm 40. The flower was dry and yellowed. Even though it had been pressed in Grams' Bible for maybe fifty years, Claire thought she could smell its faint, distant perfume.

She leaned over and kissed her Grams' cool cheek and held her hand for another minute.

Up and down the long halls, residents were falling asleep. The RN on duty was playing solitaire on a PC and didn't bother to look up as Claire walked by, exiting through the sliding glass doors.

China Bowl

On Sunday, Claire decided to go to church with Karl just to get the lay of the land and maybe discover what the big attraction was. Nu Life Pentacostal Tabernacle did not resemble anything from the Bible. It was not the big portable tent the Israelites carried through the Judean wilderness. Instead, it was a former Food Lion grocery store they'd spent a boatload of money sprucing up. The canned goods aisles had been carpeted with purple carpet and filled with fifty rows of cushioned chairs. Where the fruits and vegetables had once co-habitated, enjoying the cool comfort of an automated misting system, there was a large Visitor's Center with racks of brochures about the Tabernacle's programs. In the back where the butcher had once hacked sides of beef into steaks and ribs, there was a stage with a gigantic white cross hanging against a backdrop of purple velvet drapes.

The band was tuning up and everyone was milling around. Jesus cheerfulness and goodwill was everywhere, it was almost palpable. People were friendly to Claire. They wore big smiles and *The Lord's Gym* T-shirts, carried Bibles in embroidered covers. A lot of folks knew Karl and rushed over to meet Claire and the boys. She felt like it was the first day of school, when you're not sure who's going to be in homeroom and you've dressed up trying to make a cool first impression. Her stomach churned with apprehension. Why was she so uptight among these familiar faces? Many of the people streaming into the hall she'd seen around town. She just didn't know they were Christians. They looked and acted like everyone else.

The sanctuary went dark and the stage lights came up, illuminating sparkling band instruments. A guy with shaggy hair, a mustache and a Countryman headset ran onto the stage. Two screens, left and right, unfurled, their motors whirring, and a TV show came on (not a TV show exactly but a video with a flying chrome church logo and clips of people singing, crying and hugging). Then the video transitioned to images of nature; flowers, waterfalls, mountains, oceans, sunrises, then the band cranked up, filling the old grocery store with bluesy electric guitar riffs. The scrawny kid with a *Not Of This World* T-shirt and thousand-dollar ax didn't look like Jimmy Page but he had some Zeppelinish licks. Claire was used to the slow hymns at Magnolia Street Baptist Church where she went to Vacation Bible School a couple of times, but this was contemporary Christian music, rock n' roll with uplifting lyrics. She didn't sing at first, her mouth stubbornly glued shut, but the music had too much power over her and she began to try the words on her lips. Soon she was floating down the river of emotion with everyone else. A lot of folks had their hands in the air like they were feeling a breeze or reaching up, eager to be hugged by their heavenly father.

When the singing had ended and the tithe buckets handed around, the pastor, Trent Owens, took to the stage. He was a handsome middle-aged man with good hair, like Sheila had said, and a compassionate, loving quality to his voice. He talked about Jesus as if he knew him personally, like a friend he hung out with, like how Claire and Marla hung out, just without the weed and tequila, and he promised the congregation that none of them were beyond the reach of God's love and forgiveness.

After the service, Claire went to get the boys and they met Karl out front in the unforgiving August sun.

"The pastor wants to have lunch with us," Karl announced, grinning. "We're going to meet him at China Bowl."

"We can't afford to eat out, Karl," Claire said.

"We'll put it on the Visa," Karl said. "Wouldn't be right to make the pastor pay." Sam looked up at them clutching the colorful literature he'd been given in Sunday School.

"I thought we swore off credit cards," Claire said.

"Honey, this is too important. Let's just get over to China Bowl so we can save a table."

They waited, sipped Cokes, fed the boys crackers, watched the Sunday lunch parade, and kept a lookout for the pastor. When he arrived, half the people in China Bowl called out greetings. Karl stood up, waved both arms, the pastor saw him flailing and strolled over, shaking a few hands along the way like a politician during primary season.

"Hello friends, I mean, look at these handsome boys. I mean. And you must be Claire, Karl's rib. So good to meet you, my pleasure, yes, I mean, what a good idea, China Bowl, isn't that right. This is one of my favorites, what about you, Karl, Claire? Do you like the buffet here? Maybe we should get started, what do you say?"

They slid warm white plates from the spring-loaded plate stacker and the pastor walked alongside the boys. Toby's nose was about level with the food troughs.

"They've got just about everything under the sun including fresh fruit and coconut jello. I like coconut jello, what about you boys? I'll bet you've had jello, but have you tried the coconut jello they have here? I mean. It's unique, isn't it, jello made from coconut."

They sat down with their precarious mountains of food. Up close, Claire could see acne scars on the pastor's face, but he wore makeup to smooth out his complexion. Claire felt sorry for him. One of her best friends in high school, Chuck Brown, had suffered from bad acne. She remembered the day a guy named Harold in gym class called Chuck "pizza face," how those words had stung Chuck. In retaliation, Claire had keyed Harold's custom-painted pickup. She didn't know why she thought of that as she sat across from Pastor Trent Owens, even though he did remind her of her high school biology teacher, Mr. Dobbers, who had taught her that there are some worms, like leeches, who are hermaphrodites, and she had often thought that people would be less of a threat to each other and the world if they could fertilize themselves.

Pastor Owens blessed the food and those back in the kitchen who had prepared it, the farmers who had grown it, and the land of China, where the recipes had come from, then he proceeded to dominate the conversation with fascinating foreign stories.

"In India there is no ice. I mean, no ice for your Co-Cola, no ice for anything." The boys' eyes stretched wide with disbelief. "They use elephants the way we use trucks only the driver sits behind the elephant's head, and one time while I was there an elephant went into a rage and stomped a fella, killed him, smashed him like a banana. It was in the papers. But India is fast becoming a world superpower. They have a billion people, I mean. And nuclear bombs. And did you know they are building nuclear power plants all over India. Won't be long before they are as big and powerful as we are, with a billion people and nuclear power and bombs." Claire's meal was not settling well. She liked the pastor but she also liked peace and quiet when she ate.

"But the Indian people are the gentlest of all people, like little lambs, especially the Christians. I love them so. They treated me with so much respect. The Tabernacle gives to missions in India, did you know that? But listen to me. I'm talking too much. It's an occupational hazard I'm afraid. Claire, may I ask you something? Claire, have you given Jesus a chance to prove himself in your life?" Claire looked up from her plate, somewhat stunned, like a pink-nosed baby possum looking into the headlights of an onrushing Hummer. Her chewing slowed, slowing to a stop, she glanced at Karl from the corners of her eyes, then turned her gaze on the pastor.

"What do you mean, 'prove himself?' Didn't he do enough already. He busted out of his grave, right?"

"His tomb," Karl said.

"Same difference," Claire said. "Look, Pastor, I don't know a lot of Bible verses, but I think I'm a good person, and Karl's new interest in religion has taken us all by surprise. Two weeks ago he was passing out on the lawn."

"I understand how fast Karl has changed," Pastor Owens said. "That's just the nature of how God works for some people. But what I meant when I asked you that question was, have you given Jesus a chance to reveal himself to you personally?"

"No, I don't think I have," Claire said. "And I'm not sure I want him to."

"It won't hurt to try it," Pastor Owens said. "The reward is enormous. The reward, Claire, is eternal."

They stopped by her brother Jeb's trailer to get some cucumbers. She hadn't seen him in two weeks. He hadn't shaved and looked half-drunk. That probably meant he was having problems with Cherry, his girlfriend. She was the uncontrollable type.

"What's wrong?" Claire asked when she had him cornered in the kitchen. "Is it Cherry?"

"She ain't showed up yet from work yesterday. I think she's gone for good. I could get more loyalty from a pound mutt. Maybe that's what I need for company. I swear to God I think I should give up women."

"Well, you know what I think of her."

"No, not really."

"Cheerleading can be a curse. In high school, she was just too pretty for her own good. And look what it did. She became a stripper, then exotic lingerie, then meth smoker. I'm telling you, Jeb, she was always headed somewhere painful. Marla cheered with her, she'll tell you."

"If only I knew where she was, and if she was safe. I

40

love her, that's my damn problem."

"I'll help you look for her if you want," Karl said. He'd been listening in from the living room where the boys were planted in front of Jeb's big screen TV with Playstation controllers in their quick-fingered paws.

"That'd be great, Karl," Jeb said.

"Let's go," Karl said. "Do you mind, honey?"

"No, you two go on. I'll take the boys home in a while."

Karl came in about nine as the fireflies were beginning their poor man's laser show. Claire had already put the boys down and was watching Morley Shafer on 60 Minutes. It just happened to be about evangelicals and how they were all concerned about getting left behind when the rapture comes, and how they had voted for Bush because he was one of them.

"We found her. It took a while. We hit just about every tavern in the county."

"Where was she?"

"At her friend's house in Clinton."

"Her friend?"

"Yeah, some girl who wasn't very nice. Cherry wasn't very nice either. They were all jacked up on crystal."

"How's Jeb taking it?"

"Not so good. I think its about time he found a new girlfriend, don't you?"

"I'd say so," Claire said, shaking her head. "Poor Jeb."

"I told him we'd pray for him."

"You'd do that for Jeb? What'd he say?"

"He said he'd appreciate it."

Claire spent the rest of the evening thinking about what the pastor had said and what had happened to Jeb. She also thought about the people in India riding elephants and wondered if she would ever ride one or if she ever wanted to. She thought about how Karl had changed. He was not even like the man she married, he was better than the old Karl, new and improved, like a cordless phone or a car with GPS or a solar powered turtle light from Big Lots like the one she'd placed among the perennials. The next day he would start the job and they would have benefits and a steady check. They could pay off their credit cards, buy some things they needed at an extra fifteen percent off, and have a normal life. Now it was her turn to face the music, to face the Jesus question. Why had her family avoided church? Why didn't her mother and father ever talk about God? What was wrong with Jeb? He seemed as lost as she was. Was it a family curse? Maybe it was time to look in the mirror. Maybe it was time to give Jesus a chance to prove himself.

She and Karl made love that night, their way of celebrating the job. She wanted to give him a happy send off. Before going to sleep, Karl knelt beside the bed, folded his hands under his chin. He whispered his prayers while Claire stared at the ceiling. She decided she would get up and fix him pancakes, and set the alarm for 6:30.

As promised, Walmart put Karl to work in Tire n' Lube.

Even before he went to work for them, Claire had thought of Walmart as her home away from home. She and J.J. had spent countless hours there, and, because it was a Walmart Super Center, anything you really needed you could find there, and, if you couldn't find it, you didn't really need it. A full quarter of the employees were friends of hers, casual acquaintances, and neighbors, or faces so familiar they counted as neighbors.

Claire loved Walmart. For her and her friends growing up it was the closest thing to a mall, a place where they could gather to work on life skills. In the parking lot, on weekends, kids engaged in a lot of such practicing. The old man responsible for cleaning the wasteland on Monday embraced the nasty chore as if the trash held anthropological value. Scores of used condoms littered the asphalt, accompanied by hundreds of cigarette butts and beer bottle caps. So go the vicissitudes of a small southern town in the throes of NAFTA and unfettered teen spirit.

As Claire chased and dragged her sons through the Super Center one Tuesday afternoon, a customer in electronics started to sing. She was a young girl in dreadlocks and she sang loud as if she was on stage in a theater. Other customers stopped to watch, a crowd gathered, mystified, nobdy smiling, because it was strange, even though the song was upbeat. Soon others came from lingerie and housewares and toys, singing the same song, and dancing to pre-arranged choreography. There were twenty people altogether, singing a Walmart musical in the middle of the store, but the lyrics were farsical, condemning the mega-chain for exploiting foreign manufacturers, using child labor, and destroying local economies like the drug, hardware and grocery stores that had been put out of business in Newton Grove within a month of the Super Center's grand opening.

At the end of the song, everyone stood still, like mannequins. There was no applause. One of the performers shouted at them:

"You people are brainwashed, like zombies! Think, people, think! Walmart is your slavemaster. What does that make you?" Glaring at their blank faces, his energy waned. "Think, people," he muttered sadly before motioning to his colleagues.

Claire raced out to the parking lot as the flash mob team retreated to their tour bus. They called themselves *Voice of Young America*, and they were an anti-consumer group funded by *People for a New America*. Claire was confused, because she'd always thought Walmart was about as American as you could get. Now she was part of the Walmart family, and she didn't appreciate out-of-staters bad-mouthing her kin like those singers had done.

The days with Karl at work were a lot more boring. She had nobody to fight with, the day had no emotional charge to it, the soap operas became more vacuous than usual, it was insanely hot, the boys just stayed filthy because she didn't have the energy to bathe them or comb their hair. She might have had more energy if she hadn't been toking morning, noon and night. Once in a while she would hose the boys down and hose herself down. It was so hot outside one day in July she scalded herself with the first gush of water.

One afternoon Claire and the boys came home after a quick run to Walmart and there was a black man sitting on the front stoop. He was a young man dressed nicely in shiny shoes, tan slacks, a white shirt and a tie. A Jehovah's Witness was Claire's first thought, but they usually traveled in pairs.

"My name is George Jeffers. I'm with child protection," he said. "DSS."

"I gotta put these groceries away," Claire said, not too happy about seeing a black man from the Department of Social Services on her doorstep. She would have much preferred a Jehovah's Witness.

"Let me help bring your groceries inside," he said.

Since Sam and Toby were too little to carry anything much, Claire said, "Sure, that's great," even though now the neighbors would see a black man carrying groceries into their mobile home and might start to wonder.

Five minutes later she was standing in the kitchen. George was watching her go through the bags, and she realized he was taking a mental survey of what she had bought.

"I'm not stupid. I know what you're doing."

"Can I help put things away?" he asked. Claire was impressed with his gentle demeanor. She thought he might be gay he had such a softness to his personality.

"I've about got all the cold stuff put up," Claire said. "You want a soda? We've got Coke and root beer. No orange soda, sorry."

"Not all black people like orange soda."

"Really? Well, that's good I guess, since I don't have any."

"A Coke, please," George said. Claire opened a fresh bottle of Coke and poured him a glassful over ice.

"What'd they send you over here for?" Claire asked. "Where's Sue?"

"She quit. She's moving to Wilmington to take a job there."

"Wow, I bet she's happy about that."

"They gave me some of her cases. It looks like she was about halfway through her observation."

"She came over here twice. Both times everything went real smooth. I guess she wrote it all in my file." George already had her file open on the kitchen table.

"It says here, what you told her, was that you spanked your four-year-old with a plastic bat and that's what made the welts on his legs."

"That's right."

"But you know now that was not a good thing to do, right?"

"Well, it's not a regular habit. I don't know why the hell that lady at Burger King made it her business."

"Okay. I guess what happened is the lady at Burger King reported it to a policeman and he came to the home, and, when you came to the door, he reported you were drunk and/or stoned on drugs. So I guess that's one thing that complicated your case when it came to our office. Drugs and drinking in the home are the biggest catalysts for child abuse everywhere in America and probably the world. It's just huge."

"So what do you want me to say?" Claire needed a cigarette but wasn't about to light one up and cause a second-hand smoke cancer hazard in front of the social worker.

"I can see here what you told Sue. But the question is are you and/or your husband still getting high?"

"No. And he got a job. Plus he's a Christian now."

"Well, that's good. The job should relieve some of the stress in the home."

"He's just started at Walmart, so now we've got some benefits."

"Walmart? Well, that's good. A lot of our clients are working there. Okay then, I need to spend a few minutes talking with your boys."

"Go right ahead, you're not gonna find any more welts, unless it's something they did to their own selves." George sat on the sofa and made small talk with Toby and Sam. He looked at their arms and legs for bruises and red marks.

"It looks like they've been out in the sun," George said.

"Well, they are little boys. They like to play outdoors."

"You use sunscreen don't you?" George asked.

"Always," Claire lied. Toby looked at her, kept his mouth shut. This was the first time a black man had touched him. George's hands were thick and soft, he lifted Toby's arm delicately and looked at the white underside.

"This looks like a burn," George said.

"Yeah, he got that at my brother's garage."

"Maybe they shouldn't be in a dangerous place like a garage. How did this burn happen?"

"He touched a hotplate. My brother had popped some popcorn for them to snack on. They was just over there watching TV one afternoon, that's all."

"Popcorn?" George said, his eyes questioning.

"That's right, like one of those silver puff-up foil popper things," Claire explained.

"You mean, Jiffy Pop?" George asked. He looked into Toby's eyes. "That's what happened, huh sport?" Toby nodded his head. Claire didn't like the social worker disbelieving her.

"Where were you, Mrs. Craddock? I mean, why did you need to leave them at your brother's garage?"

"I needed a sanity break. How much longer are you people gonna be observing us?" Claire asked.

"Until the substantiation period is completed."

"How long is that?"

"At least three visits, but it can go up to five or six. We'd rather be thorough, and avoid taking the case to court, if at all possible. How have your parenting classes been going?" He stood up.

"Fine," Claire said.

"Do you have your attendance sheet?" he asked. The attendance sheet had been stuck in a drawer with their bills and other mail. George stepped beside her, so close she could smell his breath, too close, maybe he was trying to flirt or something. She glanced up at him. He was looking at her hair, then his eyes shifted to the drawer where she was fumbling through letters and sales receipts and bread ties. A sleeve of ZigZag rolling papers peeked up at her from under an envelope. She used her hand to conceal it and handed the attendance sheet to the social worker. He studied it and handed it back.

"Okay. Things are looking pretty good here. Any questions?"

"No. Well, maybe. Can I ask you a favor? When you come back again would you mind waiting for us in back of the trailer?"

"Why would I need to do that?"

"Because I don't want my neighbors wondering who you are. They might think you're someone you aren't."

"Oh, I see. Like your drug dealer?"

"No, drug dealers don't usually wear ties and tassel loafers. I mean like something else. I'm married you know," Claire reminded him.

He smiled. "Like a *boyfriend?*"

"Something like that," Claire said. "These people around here can talk."

"And I'm a black man," George said as if the racial side of it was more important than the male aspect.

"Yes you are," Claire assured him.

"Okay. Sure, I understand," George said, realizing it was a benign matter to her. "But don't you think people will be suspicious about me going around back of your house? I might get shot by some hotheaded redneck."

"I hadn't thought about that," Claire admitted. "Oh hell, sit on the stoop for all I care. Let 'em wonder."

After two weeks of Walmart employment, they used some of Karl's first paycheck to buy passes to the Newton

Grove Swim Club. Claire lay in the sun, drenched in oil, day after day, until she was dark as a Croatan. Unlike most redheads, she tanned up nicely though she suspected it would give her skin cancer down the road.

She met a woman named Blanche who had a horse farm and wedding business. All Blanche did for a living was give kids riding lessons and collect rental payments for her gazebo. She said it was too hot for lessons or weddings in August, so she hung out at the pool and drank Coronas. Blanche didn't have any kids and said she didn't want any. She said the world was too fucked up and she was too selfish. Claire wondered what she did with herself all day. Blanche didn't have a boyfriend and said she didn't even like men. Claire thought that might be because Blanche was divorced. She imagined what it would be like to have all day to herself, all night to herself. No one else to worry about, no kids to scramble your brains. Time to read books, like Marla did.

Claire invited Blanche to church. Blanche visited once and then told Claire by the pool one afternoon that she didn't believe in God. She was an atheist.

"Atheism is freedom, absolute freedom. No God to worry about, no pretending about what comes next, about life after this one. It brings you down to earth."

"What about Jesus? Don't you believe he was the Son of God?" Claire asked.

"No. Maybe he was a prophet or something, a teacher, a good man in his day, but that's all."

Blanche's point of view shocked Claire. It made her think. She remembered Pastor Owens preaching that Jesus set you free. Did she want to be free? Did she need to be free? Free from what? Free from whom? Blanche said she was free and she didn't believe in anything. Blanche was free from everything, even God.

Claire went to see the pastor. He had allotted an hour in his schedule. She came to his office but he explained that he didn't meet with women alone in his office and suggested they sit in the sanctuary.

She went ahead of him while he made a phone call. The sanctuary was usually noisy with people and music. Claire felt like the church had been deserted. She didn't even feel God's presence, nothing holy or special, it was just a dark, silent hall. On the stage there was a beautiful baby grand. She sat down on the bench and let her fingers brush the keys, then she began to play.

"What's that song?" Pastor Owens asked when he entered the sanctuary a few minutes later.

"Something my Grams taught me when I was real little. I don't know its name. I haven't played the piano in ages."

"Why not?" He settled into a chair.

"Can't afford one." Claire came down the stage stairs to join him.

"Well, you can come here and play that big black one anytime you please."

She sat down, feeling weak and stupid, the pastor moved away to put a polite empty chair between them. It was quiet, almost spookily quiet now. She couldn't remember why she'd felt compelled to make the appointment, and now she wished she hadn't come.

"What did you want to talk about, Claire?" The pastor was holding his knee with overlapped hands.

"I guess what I wanted to ask is how you're supposed to know that God and Jesus are real."

"Is that what you're struggling with?" His voice was gentle and compassionate.

"Yes. That's what I want to know."

"Well. We have to begin by taking the scriptures as being authentic, based on the scholarship. But I guess the answer to your question is that, bottom line, we can't know for sure about the reality of God or Jesus. It's something we decide to believe, we believe and take it on faith. That's what faith is, believing in what we can't see."

"I think that's hard to do," Claire said. "For me it's real hard."

"It can be hard. I mean, yes, it can be very difficult. But you can know God is real another way ... by the way he speaks to your spirit. You simply know it inside because you begin to feel his love."

"Okay."

"Do you sense God is speaking to your heart?"

"Sort of. Sometimes." She looked up at the pastor. His face seemed so kind and loving, almost beyond human. Suddenly she felt her emotions well up, like a fountain that had been stopped up and was suddenly unstopped up. She fought to keep from crying.

"Through Jesus, God has offered you forgiveness, Claire. Forgiveness for everything you ever did that was wrong or that you are ashamed of, things done to you, things that hurt you, forgiveness for all that. Do you want forgiveness?" Claire couldn't speak. Something was blocking her vocal chords. She just nodded her head. Then she began to weep uncontrollably.

Pastor Owens took her hand between his and led her in the Sinner's Prayer.

Lilly

As they drove to the Ingram's house, a Sheriff's cruiser blew past, siren blaring.

"Damn," Karl said, "wonder if he's goin' to join the search."

Claire didn't reply, she was watching the slender pines swish by, mile after mile of them, and thinking about how easy it was to get lost in the sandhills. Just because they're called "sandhills" doesn't mean there's sand everywhere. The sand was leftover from twenty million years ago when the ocean reached more than a hundred miles inland, now the area was covered with Loblolly and Virginia pines and sprawling farms growing peaches, cotton, tobacco, corn and peanuts.

Suzie and Howard Ingram had a daughter, Lilly, who was in Toby's class at Pembroke Elementary. Lilly had wandered into the woods sometime after breakfast that morning, and now people were out searching for her. When Claire heard about it at the Scotsman, she decided to go over and try to help. Karl wanted to go, too, and they had dropped the boys off with her parents.

When they got to the Ingram's, cars were parked up and down the road for a quarter mile. The fire department had hauled in the Search & Rescue trailer and a bunch of firemen were gathered at the hood of a crash truck, where they were studying grid maps. Volunteers stood around in groups waiting for instructions. The auxiliary had set up a tent and the women were handing out hot coffee and peach turnovers that had been baked at the fire department and brought over to keep everyone's blood sugar in check. There were a lot of somber faces among the people, all of whom were friends, neighbors and folks from across the county, faces Claire recognized to one degree or another, even some folks from the Tabernacle. There were farmers, business owners, house builders, and the produce man from Sav-A-Lot. Sheriff Clancy and a half dozen deputies were directing traffic and doing their best to manage the parking situation.

Karl left Claire behind and joined the crowd of volunteers. She saw Pastor Owens walking from the Ingram's house, his head bent low. He wore a sad, dejected countenance and seemed glad to see her.

"It's good to see you, Claire," he said quietly, the way you do in a funeral home even though they were standing by themselves in the Ingrams' front yard. "Do you know the family?"

"I see Suzie at the elementary some, but I don't really know her that well."

"Hmmm, I was just in the house visiting with her. I know the Ingrams don't go to our church but I thought I would pay a visit before joining the search effort. You know, times like this are so difficult, and as difficult as it is for the mother and father, as heart-breaking as it is, these good folks who have come out to assist their neighbors in a time of crisis, for them it is difficult also, I mean, there is a great weight on everyone knowing that the little girl is out there in the woods, and the cold of evening coming on within a few hours, and no sign of her at all. I heard that some of the officials are thinking she could have been abducted by a pedophile. Now we have that awful possibility running through our minds as well. Oh, dadgummit, listen to me, talking so negative, where is my faith?"

"No, it's okay," Claire said. She suddenly wished she hadn't come. She shifted her feet and looked into the pastor's sad eyes – she had been studying his face the whole time and was sharing a great foreboding of impending tragedy, as if she had entered a dark and frightening tunnel.

"She could use you in there," the pastor said, nodding toward the house. "She could use someone strong to lean on." Claire didn't think of herself as strong, but she said "okay" and began walking toward the door.

It seemed like all the lights were on inside and she saw women milling around. The front door was ajar and Claire noticed how the carpeting inside the door had been soiled by people tramping on it. She thought the chatter of the women was way too lively under the circumstances. That was her first impression. There were at least a dozen women in the living room socializing like they were at a Tupperware party. She looked around for Suzie Ingram. Seemed like nobody was in charge.

She saw an open door down a dark hallway, walked into the hallway and came to a bathroom with goldfish swimming on the wallpaper. There was another door at the end of the hallway that was closed, and she expected it was the bedroom. She knocked lightly and heard Suzie say, "It's open." She turned the doorknob carefully as if she was unlocking a safe, but then she saw Suzie curled up on the queen-size bed and realized nothing was safe about this room. Suzie's eyes were red and teary. She sat up, a pillow pressed against her spine.

"Don't I know you?" she asked. "From Lilly's school?"

"Yeah, my boy Toby goes there. He's in her class."

"That's why you came to see me?" she asked.

"I wanted to do something. Can I get you anything?"

"Only if you can get my little girl back." Claire sat on the edge of the bed. Suzie pulled her knees up and pressed her face against them, her sobbing soft and muffled. Claire didn't know what to do or say. After a minute, Suzie got up and said, "Let's make some coffee."

They went into the kitchen. The countertop was covered with food. Casseroles, cakes, pies, boxes of Bojangles chicken, a big tub of Walmart potato salad, you name it. Suzie got the bag of Folgers out of the refrigerator. Claire knew that some people kept their coffee in there to keep it fresh but she kept hers in the cabinet. She and Karl preferred Coke anyway and she only made coffee when J.J. came over. Suzie scooped the white filter full of coffee while Claire filled the machine with water up to the ten cup limit.

"Look at all this goddamn food," Suzie said, "it makes me feel like we're already having a funeral. I don't know where all these people came from."

"I thought they were your friends," Claire said.

"I don't have any real friends here," Suzie said. "We just moved here two years ago from Ohio, but, I guess some of these people think they're my friends, some of them live around here, but all my real friends are back in Ohio."

"I guess people don't know what to do, but they want to help."

"I know," Suzie said, and that's all she seemed able to say, so for a minute they listened to the coffee pot gurgle and drip. "I can be a real asshole. I've been promising God I'll stop being such an asshole if he'll just bring my Lilly back."

"You don't seem like an asshole kind of person to me," Claire said.

"Thanks. But I am. I treat Howie like shit. I even treat Lilly like shit sometimes. It's because I have unresolved issues, that's what everybody says, issues from my childhood.

"Unresolved issues? Like what?"

"I don't know, like a real strict mom and dad. They were real strict religious people, practically lived at the church, always searching for something more out of God and Jesus and all that bullshit."

"You don't believe in any of that?" Claire asked.

"I don't know what to believe, but if he takes my Lilly away from me, I will hate him forever, because how could God do that if he loves me. And if he loves Lilly."

"Do you want some coffee?" Claire asked. She poured them both a cup and put milk and sugar in hers. Suzie just took milk.

Claire followed Suzie onto the screened-in back porch. Lilly's toys were strewn about on the artificial grass floor. The toys looked lonely, like they were begging for a child to come and play with them. Then Claire remembered seeing Suzie at Walmart at Christmas. The memory came back vividly, like a movie. She had run into her in the toy section. Suzie had probably bought some of these toys that day. Claire noticed that it had gotten darker outside, then she realized that the screens surrounding the porch were tarnished black and made the forest beyond look darker than it really was. Claire thought about reminding Suzie that they had seen each other at Walmart but then decided against it, thinking it might make her sadder, and make her cry again. They heard laughter coming from the living room, trailing from there through the kitchen and onto the back porch. It made Claire mad.

"Shit," Suzie muttered.

"Do you want me to ask them to keep it down?" Claire asked.

"I wish you'd ask them to leave," Suzie said.

When Claire spoke to the women, they didn't seem to be offended, except for one, who acted put off but didn't voice it. Claire returned to the porch where she and Suzie sat in plastic chairs and watched the search operation in the cow pasture about a hundred yards away.

Soon they could feel the chill of the evening come on, and Claire knew that Suzie was thinking about Lilly and how Lilly was feeling the same chilly air that had seeped onto the darkening porch. Claire turned on a light and moths began to grip the screen, flutter and bang against it, then grip it again, wanting more of the glowing bulb.

The moon appeared, high over the pines and almost transluscent. Some of the searchers returned. As each two-man team emerged from the black woods, Suzie took a deep breath in anticipation.

Claire saw three men coming toward the house from

the parking area. One of them was the Indian she had seen at the Inferno. He was taller than the other two. They all wore camo green BDU pants and down vests with T-shirts underneath. As they came closer, Claire went out the porch door and stood on the stoop waiting for them.

The tall man introduced himself as Storm Eagle, then introduced his friends. They were named Bent Arrow and Sam. He glanced at Suzie standing as motionless as a statue behind the porch screen. Claire could see how concerned he was – his eyes were tense, his voice serious. Suzie watched them for a minute then disappeared into the kitchen.

A minute later, Claire walked into the house and found Suzie sitting at the kitchen table eating a Mrs. Smith's chocolate pie with her finger. "He wants to know where you saw Lilly last," Claire said.

They walked into the yard and Suzie showed them the spot where Lilly had been playing. She had been practicing the hula hoop, Suzie said. Then the men began studying the ground and walked into the woods together.

"Who are they?" Suzie asked.

"They're Croatans. Storm Eagle, the big guy, said that his friends are sign cutters. A sign cutter is a professional tracker. Storm Eagle knows how to track, too, but he said the other guys are the best trackers in both Carolinas."

"It's pitch dark out there in the woods. Why'd they wait so long?"

"Sam had to drive down from Asheville. Anyhow, Storm Eagle said it was better to track at night because with their flashlights they can see the shadow a footprint makes. They're going to go all night if they have to. He said to tell you that."

"Do you mind staying?" Suzie asked.

"No, I don't mind," Claire said, "the boys are with Momma and Daddy.

Karl returned from walking a second grid and came looking for Claire. By then, she and Suzie were sitting in the living room with the TV on. They had watched the six o'clock news, then Suzie had fallen asleep.

"You take the car and pick up the boys, I'll stay here with Suzie," she told him. Karl was pleased that she wanted to stay. He thought this was the best thing they had ever done as a couple other than bring the boys into the world, but he was pretty sure they would find the girl dead. That's what most of the people outside were saying now, and, when he told Claire, she started to cry. He held her for a moment and stroked her hair. She rubbed her wet eyes on his shirt. She could see he was worn out. She was proud of him and kissed his sweaty cheek before turning away to go back inside.

Later that evening, around eight, Claire and Suzie walked over to see what was happening with the search and rescue teams. Out of respect, everyone became quiet when they saw Suzie. The dog teams had just started to arrive. Some of them had come from as far away as Charlotte and Greensboro. They were getting the rundown from the incident commander, a guy named Jake Johnson who had been a volunteer fireman for over thirty years and drove an F150 painted the color of a fire engine, with a light bar on top, a winch and everything else he might need, including the jaws of life, which he kept in a special toolbox in the bed. He walked over to Suzie and put his hand on her shoulder.

"We are extending the search and bringing in the dogs. I have a good feeling about this, Suzie. Can't make any promises, except to promise our very best effort. Got a ton of people come out to help. Now, the dog boys need to talk to you, is that alright?" Suzie nodded, and Jake motioned to a couple of men standing nearby. They came over and introduced themselves. One was named Benny and he was old with a grizzled face, the other was a lanky black man named Zeb.

"We'll need to go into the house and get something to scent off of," Benny said. Sheriff Clancy came over, too, and they all went inside. Claire would learn later that the dog teams always asked a law enforcement person to accompany them inside, since they were often searching for drugged or intoxicated people and the lifestyle circumstances could be problematic. She would also learn that one of the dog teams specialized in finding the bodies of missing people. They were called *cadaver dogs.*

The men went into Lilly's bedroom and looked around. They put on rubber gloves. They decided to take the pink pajama shirt Lilly had worn the night before, and the insoles from a pair of her sneakers. The men smelled of cigars and English Leather, wood smoke and hotdog chili.

"We've got a lot of food if you want anything," Claire said.

"Thanks anyway, ma'am, we're ready to get started."

As the men were leaving, Suzie's husband, Howie, came

in. He was flat wore out but highly adrenalized by fear of losing his little girl.

"Come here a minute," Sheriff Clancy said to him and they walked into the kitchen. Claire and Suzie sat in the living room again and from where she was sitting she could see the Sheriff pouring Howie a finger of bourbon from a silver flask. The Sheriff was also offering some words of encouragement.

Around 11:00 o'clock, Claire walked outside by herself and smoked a cigarette. There were even more people taking part in the search, probably because it had been on the news and people were driving in from surrounding counties. She got a cup of coffee and ate a donut and talked to the auxiliary ladies. She could hear indistinct voices chattering across the field and the dot matrix printers inside the firemen's vehicles spitting out grid maps. The searchers moved in the glow of halogen worklights, dozens of silhouetted shapes, their breaths punctuating the cool air, drifting in bluish beams of light. She was tired and went inside. She put as much of the food away as she could find room for in the refrigerator, then she fell asleep on the living room sofa.

The Ingram house faced east and undammed sunlight splashed through the windows the next morning, awaking Claire at seven fifteen. Howie was already up and had gone outside. Claire made coffee and took a cup to Suzie, who had slept in her clothes, her hair bunched and lopsided when she sat up in bed.

"I shouldn't of said that about God." Suzie took a sip of steaming coffee. "He's going to hate me for it."

"Why would you say that? He won't hate you."

"Claire, I had a horrible dream. I dreamed they found Lilly in a stream, and she was dead. But the stream ran into a place, like a whirlpool, where the water went spiralling down into the earth, and even in my dream I knew that was hell, and my little girl was going to be sucked down into it if I didn't do something, but I didn't know what to do." Suzie cried, perhaps relieved that her dream wasn't true but also realizing that the chance of finding Lilly alive was becoming more and more remote.

"Would you like to walk outside in a few minutes?" Claire asked. "I think the searchers would like to see you."

"Why would they want to see me?"

"Because they're doing this for you, to bring your girl back to you."

"Okay," Suzie said, and after she washed her face and changed clothes, they went outside. The day was fresh and cool. It was only eight o'clock. They could hear dogs baying in the distance, probably the cadaver dogs run by Carolina Canine Rescue.

When they got to the staging area, a news crew had just arrived from Raleigh. They were angling their motorized Trackstar satellite antanae into space. The news girl approached to introduce herself. Behind them, the searchers and firemen began to applaud.

At the far end of the pasture, Storm Eagle and his friends appeared through the grey mist. Storm Eagle was carrying Lilly in his arms and she was alive. Suzie ran to them and the crowd closed in, surrounding the Indians and

Suzie and Howie as they hugged their daughter. The news crew was videotaping the event. Some of the firefighters were shaking their heads in disbelief. Claire sank to her knees and cried.

A few minutes later, she was drinking coffee with Storm Eagle and he was telling her how they had found Lilly curled up in leaves trying to keep warm, and how she had walked in an almost straight direction for three and a half miles. She hadn't said why she walked away from home, and he hadn't asked her, but he said he could tell she was an unhappy child, because she had an unsettled spirit.

Storm Eagle was the kind of man Claire wished she had married instead of Karl. Even the way he held his coffee cradled in his huge hands, and the hands, dark, rugged, hard-working hands, somehow turned her on. The way he looked at her made her think that he liked her, because he kept glancing at her hair. Maybe he liked redheads. A lot of men did.

Duke

Blanche's wedding factory was named "Blueberry Knoll." Wild blueberry bushes grew abundantly in the woods surrounding the knoll where a gazebo looked upon a lake covered in bright green algae, making it the transcendent context for wedding nuptials, a young bride's dream come true.

Blanche's ex-husband had built the gazebo to house a hot tub. She had sold the hot tub and painted the whole thing white with yellow trim. At dusk, when wrapped in ribbons and a thousand miniscule white lights, the gazebo was a spectacular sight. Blanche was able to get a grand for her wedding package. (She also had a party tent and a patio for receptions and a guesthouse that was used by the bride and her maids for dressing themselves and lying in wait.)

At Blanche's request, Claire dropped by on a Friday afternoon to help her prepare for a Saturday ceremony.

"This is a horrible weekend for a wedding," Blanche said. "The cake is going to melt." She was scrubbing trampled frosting from the patio floor using a stiff-bristled industrial broom and soapy water. She stopped and rested her chin on the end of the broom handle, gazing down at Claire, who was touching up white tent poles with a small paint brush.

"Claire, do you want to know why I hate men?"

"Why, Blanche?"

"Because they are so very disappointing. I've never actually met a whole, mature, fully male man. I don't think they exist. Maybe we've simply emasculated them to death, maybe we've turned real men into an endangered species." Claire wasn't sure what emasculated meant but she nodded her head anyway. "Or maybe it's just living in the sticks where the only thing men care about is bass fishing and deer hunting and racing their lawnmowers. What do you think?"

"Karl used to be a lot of fun," Claire said, pensively dipping the brush into the quart of paint. "Now he's born again and not much fun, but it's better because he would've killed himself, and maybe me along with him."

"He ever hit you?"

"Lots of times, I hate to admit."

"I'm sorry, Claire."

"I have good resistance to pain. Maybe that's why I don't hate men like you do."

"Oh, I see, you are tailor-made for abuse. The perfect punching bag. That makes a lot of sense, Claire, a whole lot of sense. You frighten me." Blanche squirted another stream of soap onto the concrete, shaking her head, amazed. "You really frighten me."

The Saturday wedding was blistering, but the bride and groom didn't seem to care. Claire could see they were in lust, dreaming about their honeymoon in Aruba, and unconcerned about the damp discomfort of their entourage. Like a horsefly on the wall, Claire watched them, buzzed from place to place, served punch, carried more ice to the bar, assisted the caterers when asked.

During the reception, the bride went inside the guesthouse to change into her honeymoon outfit and wouldn't come out. Her bridesmaids went in to see her and huddled with the bride's mother. Claire could overhear them.

"She's changed her mind," her mother said. "She doesn't want to be married to him anymore."

"This has to be the shortest marriage ever," one of the bridesmaids said without realizing she'd made a bad joke.

"Can I talk to her?" Claire asked. The mother looked her in the face for the first time that day.

"Who are you? You're the serving girl. What the hell, go ahead."

Claire entered the dressing room. The bride was seated at the window. She'd been crying, her makeup streaked and smudged like her dreams. She looked up but Claire's presence didn't seem to surprise her.

"Hi," Claire said.

"Hey. What's up?" the bride sputtered.

"You got everybody freaked out."

"I'm kinda freaked out myself."

"Everybody's wondering what happened."

"You want me to tell you what happened? I don't even know you."

"Maybe I can help somehow."

"I seriously doubt it. But I'll tell you anyway. I'm so embarrassed. But I can't stay married to that asshole."

"What happened?" Claire touched the bride's trembling

hand.

"Just a minute ago, I saw my *husband* making eyes at Jennifer Andrews. And the thing is, I always knew he had a thing for her, for as long as I've known him. Then he has the gall to dance with her. And when they're dancing she looks over at me and winks. Can you fucking believe that?"

"I'll tell you what I'd do," Claire said. "I'd ask her to go for a walk with me, and I'd walk down by the pond. Along the way I'd tell her how nice it is she's my husband's friend and how her and you should be friends now and crap like that. Then, when I got to the bridge, I'd give her a big hug, and I'd push her into the water."

"You'd do that?"

"Yep."

"What about Larry?"

"Who's that?"

"My *husband.*"

"I'd take a wait n' see approach to him. He's probably been emasculated."

"You're probably right," the bride said. "Okay, I'll do it." She was suddenly giddy.

Claire ran to get Blanche and they watched the scene unfold. The bride did exactly what Claire had told her to do. There was only one hitch – when Jennifer Andrews hit the lake, she began floundering in her dress and started to drown. A half dozen men came to her rescue, adding far more drama to the stunt than Claire had expected.

Claire and Blanche sat around drinking leftover wine and eating wedding cake for an hour after the guests had departed, re-envisioning the scene again and again, laughing their heads off until a stream of wine gurgled out Claire's nose. The best part of it was that so many disposable Kodak cameras were flashing when Jennifer Andrews was pulled out of the lake draped in algae, her satin shoes coated with brown sludge, surrounded by a coterie of dripping men.

Monday night, Sam almost stopped breathing, and a meth lab blew up, creating all kinds of chaos at the hospital. When Claire and Karl rushed Sam into the emergency room, a teenage boy was sitting there waiting to have glass plucked out of his face. Thank God Marla was on duty, because she immediately took them back to an examination room. Sam's lungs had trouble working and the side of his face was drooping. Claire was fighting back the onrush of panic and tears. Marla laid Sam on an examination table and put him on oxygen.

"I don't know what this is," Marla said. "I'm going to call a neurologist. Dr. Jennings. Try to keep him relaxed. Try not to worry, sweetie." Marla squeezed Claire's arm reassuringly, but Claire heard the worry in her voice.

Karl paced the exam room in his blue Tire n' Lube uniform, the backs of his hands smeared with black soot and brake dust, his hair pressed into a funny shape by his cap, which had fallen off as he ran through the sliding glass emergency room doors with Sam in his arms. He stood over his four-year old, helplessly gazing down at him, feeling desperate and afraid. The church had tenderized him and made his true self accessible, but now, in this all too mortal moment, his belief in God wasn't helping. Used to be his drinking washed away his real feelings. But facing this kind of thing, for a man like Karl, was hard. He had a fierce love for his boys, yet here he was totally helpless. He'd grown up without a dad, no role model for the job of father, no orientation, and he had to rely on the love he had for the boys to motivate him. It was for them he had turned to God as much as for Claire or himself. He didn't want them to grow up with a drunken, dopehead dad.

Claire's mother and father came in. Of course J.J. was beside herself. Her nature was to take charge of a situation but there was nothing she could do for Sam except elicit a whimpering sigh from his frozen lips. Marla was on the phone trying to reach the neurologist.

"You better leave, Momma, Sam has to stay relaxed."

"Oh my baby," J.J. said. "Oh my God."

" Momma, go find some coffee for you and Daddy, the cafeteria's in the basement."

"I know where the damn cafeteria is, Claire, I birthed you in this hospital."

Two weeks had passed since Claire started to church. In that short span of time she and Karl had made some friends. They'd been to a bowling night and a picnic. But they were surprised when two dozen prayer warriors showed up at the hospital with Pastor Trent Owens at two o'clock in the morning. When Claire entered the waiting room they converged on her like honeybees around an injured queen. Right there in public they formed a circle, held hands, and lifted up Sam with healing prayers.

"Guess who's here?" Marla said, poking her head into triage a half hour later. "Cherry. She was at the meth lab. Her face is cut up and her lungs might be burned."

"Is she going to be okay?" Claire asked.

"Oh sure, it's mainly a cosmetic problem. Her lungs will heal up. And Dr. Jennings is on his way. He was at his fishing cabin. The pastor wants to come in, is that okay?"

"Do you think he should?" Karl asked, glancing at Sam, whose eyes were closed. "Sam's asleep."

"I'll tell him he can come in, but only for a minute," Marla said in a hushed tone.

A minute later, the pastor appeared at the door. "Hi all, how's our boy doing?"

"He's asleep right now, pastor," Claire whispered, "but there's something really wrong with him."

"What are the symptoms?"

"He can't swallow, he can't hardly breathe, his face is drooping, he's drooling, and his eyes are droopy, too."

"Sounds like a stroke maybe," the pastor said.

"The neurologist is coming," Karl said.

"Well there is nothing God can't handle," the pastor said. He rested his hands lightly on Sam's head. "Father, we entrust this precious one to your care. Spare his life. Heal him, Lord. Direct the doctors' hands, Lord. Take charge of his medical condition now. We ask you these things in Jesus' name, amen. Now take heart you two. I mean, God is not going to let you down."

"I hope not," Claire said.

"Thank you, pastor," Karl said.

When Dr. Jennings arrived he was wearing jeans and a

red flannel shirt. Claire noticed he smelled like a campfire. As soon as he saw Sam's face he told Marla to call Duke to send a helicopter.

"We can't treat him here. I don't think it's a stroke. I think it's myasthenia gravis."

"What's that?" Karl asked.

"A neuromuscular disorder, a condition that affects the nerves and muscles. It can be treated with medication. Right now we need to get him to the specialists at Duke. I can give him something to keep him calm."

While Marla sat with Sam, Karl and Claire went out to see their church friends and give them a report. Their friends decided to stay until the helicopter came.

As Claire and Karl looked out the windows of the helicopter they could see the crowd in the parking lot under the yellow glow of streetlamps, waving like crazy and throwing kisses.

At Duke Hospital, Claire and Karl waited for the doctors to do tests and diagnose Sam. They slept in his room and at a nearby Econo-Lodge. J.J. and Big Eddie were watching Toby. Claire called twice a day to give them updates. Walmart told Karl they would hold his job open, but when Karl checked on the status of his benefits, he found out that he had no insurance coverage for Sam.

"I did something real stupid I guess," Karl said. "They said I was supposed to sign something if wanted to have all of you guys covered in the policy." He was so bummed at himself, Claire didn't have the heart to kick him while he was down. So, they had to put everything on credit cards. J.J. and Big Eddie said they would help out even if they had to cash in some CDs or sell the motorhome. Pastor Owens told Karl the church would take up a special collection.

Claire had begun to pray even before Sam took ill and now she was praying a lot for him to get better. When she closed her eyes she could feel something comforting. Pastor Owens said God was using this trial to reveal himself to her and to prove himself powerful in her life.

Dr. Sing had a plastic brain on his desk. Actually it was a whole head but the top of the skull came off and the brain sat inside like a giant pink walnut in its shell. Claire figured Dr. Sing had a plastic brain because he was a neurosurgeon who could work on the brain if necessary even though he was treating Sam with medicine. He had asked them to meet him in his office for a consultation. Sam had been under his care for a week and was doing much better. They had grown to admire the doctor, who was an Indian man from a big city in India. He had a very smooth and polished personality, and Claire thought his skin, which was a rich cocoa color, was also smooth and polished, perfect, without a single blemish, and with only a thin black mustache. His irises were black as onyx stones. He invited them to sit across from his desk and he stood in front of them leaning on the edge of the desk. Karl noticed that his shoes and socks looked expensive. People in Newton Grove didn't wear shoes and socks like that. Karl noticed a Harvard diploma on the wall. He wondered what made some people so much smarter than others. Why did he work at Walmart and Dr. Sing at Duke? Was it in the genes? How he was raised? Just plain desire and ambition? Ever since he and Claire had walked into the hospital, life had become a mystery to him. He saw people from all over the world, with all kinds of medical problems, and doctors from India and China and one from Argentina, and he'd thought about the human body and how complicated it was, how intricate God had made it, yet it could be repaired almost like a car if you knew the manual inside and out like these guys.

"Sam is doing well don't you think?" Dr. Sing said. "He is a strong fellow."

"He's a lot better," Claire said. "We appreciate everything you've done."

"Well, it is my job, but I wanted to talk with you regarding Sam. His condition is an ongoing medical condition for his whole lifetime and he must take it easy when he returns to normal living. Also, he must eat a healthy diet. I will give diet guidelines for you to take home."

"When can we take him home?" Karl asked.

"One more week and he'll be ready to go."

"Are you a believer?" Karl asked. A Bible was sitting on Dr. Sing's desk.

"Yes I am Christian. Are you Christian?"

"We go to Nu Life Pentacostal Tabernacle," Karl said.

"When I lived in India, in my schooling years, I met a young man who had seen the Jesus movie in his village, and this man thought Jesus was a movie character. He did not know Jesus was a real person."

"That's funny," Claire said.

"Yes, I thought so, too," the doctor said. "I think many people think Jesus is a movie character, because the Mel Gibson movie was very popular, but if they would read the Bible they would see him for who he is."

"How did you become a Christian?" Claire asked.

"In India my father is the pastor of a church. Yes, and he sent me here for my schooling, and for advanced medical training. We will start a hospital in India one day."

"Our pastor, Trent Owens, travels to India," Claire said. "He said he heard a story about a man who got crushed by an elephant."

"Elephants are dangerous. People do not realize. And we have tigers in the countryside, and sometimes they attack people. But most of the time it is people getting run into by the cars that is a major problem in our cities."

"That happens here, too," Karl said. "I guess that happens everywhere."

"Would you rather be hit by a car or attacked by a tiger?" Claire asked.

"I had much rather be hit by a car," Dr. Sing said, 'but not badly hit, of course. A tiger is a bad deal. I have seen the results. Tigers have so much power for crushing in their jaws. It is a very bad deal."

Night after night, Claire sat up with Sam, and it gave her time to think. Maybe too much time, because she thought about things that went back into her childhood, like the time when J.J. took her to the beauty parlor and got her hair cut in bangs. She was ten and she looked stupid and it was the first time she felt hatred for her mother. At her birthday party when she turned twelve, Big Eddie had gotten drunk with his buddies in the backyard and the gas grill caught fire and they hooted and hollered but the burgers were burnt to a crisp. And the time in elementary school when she made out with Jack Henson inside the huge red ceramic pipe on the playground, and they didn't even know what they were doing but it made her feel good, light-headed, grown-up and wildly alive. Her childhood had been so average and she was so average, even below average, a dumb country girl who lived in a singlewide and had no real skills or talents, just a high school education and no real desire to be anything. A pretty smile and red hair don't count when it comes to job skills. A sense of humor don't count either. She was not even that good of a mother. She had lost her temper with Sam and Toby a bunch of times, smacked them, screamed at them, taken her frustrations out on them. If she kept it up, they might run away like Lilly did and die in the forest or get kidnapped by a pervert. Deep in her heart she knew she didn't deserve her boys, that she wasn't up to it. J.J. and Big Eddie hadn't raised her to be anything special, so how was she going to raise her boys to be anything special? Being at Duke had made her see the true reality. The nurses were confident, the female doctors were smart, sharp, professional. Marla had made it through nursing school but Claire didn't think she could do something like that. Marla said anatomy almost killed her. The only thing Claire thought she could be good at was being a stripper. When she stripped for Karl, he said it was good the way she stayed in time with the music. But it was not right for a mother to be doing that. Plus she might like it too much and go off the deep end. And maybe that's why she drank so much and smoked so much weed. Maybe she was trying to escape the truth about herself. In that cold, sterile hospital room, as she watched Sam sleep, and watched the news about the war in Iraq, she realized that the planet didn't need a person like her, who was *good for nothing,* the planet didn't need anybody like that, and neither did Sam or Toby or even Karl. So, she decided she would change. Even if it killed her, she would make something of herself. Next came the question, what would it be?

McGill's Gulf

Duke flew them back to Newton Grove. Dr. Sing said it would be easier on Sam than a two-hour drive. When they landed at the county hospital heliport, their friends from church were there, and J.J., Big Eddie and Toby. The EMTs allowed Toby to ride in the ambulance with his brother.

At home they found casseroles and flowers and cards, some with cash inside. Claire stopped trying to hold back her tears, sat on the sofa, and cried. She'd never felt so loved by so many. That's where she was when Marla dropped by to see Sam.

"You okay, girl?" Marla asked.

"Um-hm. Everybody's been so nice to us, I just lost it."

"Well that's understandable, you've been through a stressful time. Did I tell you what happened to Cherry? She took an overdose. As in suicide attempt."

"Oh my God. Did she die?"

"No, but she's in the psyche ward at Butner." They walked into the kitchen and Claire got them two Diet Mountain Dews.

"Have you seen Jeb lately?" Claire asked. "I was hoping he'd come by to see Sam. I talked to him a few times from the hospital but he never mentioned Cherry."

"Huh," Marla said.

"I know," Claire said. "I know."

"He must be tore up," Marla said. She took a slurping

sip of her drink and looked at Claire. "I'd like to see him myself."

"You're kidding, right?" Claire rolled her eyes. She couldn't believe her ears.

"I kinda miss him," Marla admitted. Jeb and Marla had dated all through high school and their breakup had been loud and messy.

"You don't want to go *there*, I don't think," Claire said. Marla ignored her and walked down the hallway.

"Where's our little soldier?" They went into the boys' room. Sam was sleeping soundly on the lower bunk, his brother overhead, both breathing quietly and steadily.

"You were lucky," Marla said. "Sam's illness is really serious, I guess you found that out at Duke. He could have died if you hadn't gotten to us when you did."

"We had a lot of people praying," Claire said.

"Do you really believe that did anything?" Marla asked. Claire could see it was an earnest question.

"Marla, I want to believe in something. That's not such a terrible thing to want is it?"

Claire met Karl at the Walmart to buy toys for Sam, since he was going to be stuck indoors for at least two more weeks. They walked all over the store talking about what they could use, but they only bought a shirt for each of the boys, some Lord of the Rings figures, and a board game called Catch Phrase because they were going to a game night with their church friends and didn't have any board games at home except Candyland.

Claire dropped by Tire n' Lube to say hi to Karl's fellow employees. Some of them were black, three or four Mexican. Everyone seemed happy to be there, happy to have a paycheck, plus some of the best junk food in Newton Grove was served right on the premises. Claire left thinking that Walmart was one big happy family and now she and Karl were officially part of it, and what a blessing that was. She had begun to think in terms of blessings because that was the subject of Pastor Owens' sermon on Sunday, counting your blessings, being thankful. He had used Sam's experience to illustrate his sermon. She had never not been thankful for being pretty and for the boys. Now she had become thankful for Karl again, and thankful that her life seemed to have balance. She hadn't had a fury spell in recent memory, hadn't broken her hand hitting the refrigerator or smacked the boys with a plastic bat. But she had missed her parenting classes while they were at Duke. She needed to call George and let him know what had happened to Sam.

Claire drove by her mother's but didn't stop. The boys were probably watching *The Young and The Restless* with her. It was an hour long right at noon. Something made her keep driving, and before she knew it she was pulling into the parking lot at Sampson Community College. The Newton Grove campus was new and very contemporary with modern architecture of steel and glass. She'd heard somewhere that North Carolina's community college system was one of the best in the nation, but she'd never set foot in one of the buildings. She had no idea it was so much nicer than high school, but her high school was so old the chewing gum under the desks was three layers thick – at Sampson High, vandalizing desks with wads of BubbleYum was a generational sin.

A nice grey-haired lady, like somebody's granny, talked to her and showed her the courses she could enroll in.

"What kind of degree do you want to pursue?" she asked.

"I have no idea."

"Well, there's nothing wrong with exploring your options. Maybe you should focus on what interests you."

"I don't know what interests me."

"Something in the liberal arts perhaps?"

"What's 'liberal arts'"?

"Literature, painting, pottery, music, history."

"What's available in the literature category?"

"Do you want to read it or write it?"

"I've never written anything except some poems when I was in the ninth grade."

"We have a poetry class. It's a beginner class."

"Okay, I'll take that, why not, and some history. I always liked history."

She drove to the hospital to tell Marla. Marla took a cigarette break and they stood outside on the cafeteria loading dock. An old black man was washing out big plastic trash cans with a hose.

"I signed up for History of the Native Americans and poetry," Claire said proudly.

"Aren't you the cat's meow, girl. *Poetry* and *Indians*. That's so cool."

"If you want you can come to the Tabernacle this Sunday. There's a picnic after the service."

"How could I pass that up," Marla said.

"Bring Tommy if you wanna."

"I don't know if I wanna. Is Jeb coming?" Marla asked.

"I haven't asked him."

"Is he over Cherry?"

"I don't know, want me to ask him?"

"Sure." Marla crushed out the butt of her cigarette with the white toe of her nurse's sneaker. "Ask him for me. Tell him I said I'm looking forward to seeing him."

Claire went straight to McGill's Gulf. Jeb was hoisting an engine out of an old Jeep. The garage was like her home away from home. Her Daddy had bought it in 1955, the year James Dean died crashing his Porsche 550 Spyder. In the sixties, Big Eddie had become semi-famous on the late model circuit. Before retiring, he and Jeb had built up the repair side of the station and made some good money. When Jeb and Big Eddie worked together they didn't have to pay anybody else and anyway every mechanic worth his salt had his own backyard garage or worked at Goodyear, Advance Auto, or the Chevrolet dealership in Clinton.

She picked up an oversize socket wrench and swung it around. It sounded like a rattlesnake rattling its tail. Big Eddie had never let her work in the garage even though she liked the tools and the smells of grease and engine soot. Big Eddie said she would hurt herself and sure enough one of his hired boys, Wally Pullen, got ugly second-degree burns on his chest when he opened a hot radiator. There were lots of ways to get hurt or killed in a garage and more than once her father had been happy to list them for her:

Tire explodes shooting valve stem through eye into brain

Car falls off lift crushing every bone in body

Drinking antifreeze thinking it's Mountain Dew burns hole in intestines

Hoist chain snaps and engine mashes foot flat as pancake

Car hood falls and crushes hand, maybe head

Car backing out rolls over foot, or, pulling in, crushes pelvis

Carburetor spring pops off and flies up nose to brain

Torque wrench slips in hand, breaks jaw

Welding torch blows up in face, killing instantly

Bay door crushes skull when you aren't looking

Gasoline spill burns you to a crisp when lighting cigarette

Carbon monoxide silently puts you to sleep and kills

Air gun gets out of control, whips around, punctures eyeball

Irate customer or everyday robber shoots you

"Where'd you get that?" Claire asked, pointing to the engine with the shiny handle of the socket wrench.

"Oh, hi sis. You mean the Jeep?"

"Yeah. I always wanted a Wrangler."

"I'm rebuilding it. I'll sell it cheap."

"Cheap is too high for me," Claire said. "You want a soft drink?"

"Okay," Jeb said. He kept working, cranking the hoist while Claire slid two bottles from the refrigerated case and brought them over.

"Can you stop that for a minute?" she asked. The engine twisted gracefully in midair.

"What? Something on your mind?" Jeb swigged from his bottle of Cheerwine.

"How ya doin'?" Claire asked.

"I'm okay."

"Seein' anybody?" Jeb looked at the engine. It had quit swinging. He was using the moment to think about Cherry and how much her hurting him still stung.

"I don't want to see anybody for a while," he said soberly.

"Why not?"

"Cause there ain't anybody worth the time in this shithole town. Hey, you gotta see something." Jeb took her to the freezer chest in the office where he kept surplus ice cream and frozen dinners for when he worked late. He opened the lid. There under a swaddle of plastic was some kind of furry animal.

"What is it?"

"It's a wolf pup," Jeb said.

"Oh my god," Claire said. "Where'd you get it?"

"I shot it."

"Why in the world would you shoot a baby wolf like that?" Claire's impulse was to reach out and pet it, but it was covered in freezer snow. She brushed some aside. "I saw this little guy the other night. He was standing in the middle of the bridge." The wolf's fur was a reddish-gold color, the same color as her hair when she was a little girl. She stroked the white fur under its chin. "He's so pretty."

"I didn't know it was a puppy. I thought it was a stray dog or fox trying to terrorize my rabbits." He let the lid fall closed with a smack. "Oh well. I felt awful about it, believe me, sis."

"Why'd you put it in your freezer?

"Thought I'd get it stuffed, stick it in the front window, let it welcome the customers."

"That's a good idea. This place could use a little wolf in the window." Claire slipped her bottle into the last empty slot in the wooden crate. "You wanna come to the Tabernacle Sunday, we're having a picnic lunch."

"This Sunday?"

"Um-hm."

"Sure. Why not. Is it a dress up deal?"

"No, casual. We're a come-as-you-are-church."

"Come as I are?" he said, looking at the grease on his forearms.

"Well, take a shower. And put on some smell good, okay." Jeb chugged the last of his drink.

"Is that what you come here for, to ask me to church?" Jeb had quizzical look in his eyes. Claire bit her lip.

"Marla's going to be there."

"Marla?"

"Yes, Marla."

"What are you tryin' to do, sis? I don't know about

this."

"I'm gonna call you Sunday morning. You better not get drunk Saturday night. Jeb, you gotta promise." He just looked at her. "Hey, I didn't even know you still had any rabbits," Claire said on her way to the pumpkin.

Other than Jesus Christ himself, there's probably no better reason for joining a big country church than their covered dish dinners. After loud singing (to a full rock n' roll band), joyful worship with dazzling multimedia, and a firey sermon, there's just nothing better than those long tables piled with food made by the loving hands of little old grandmas and big-hipped farm women.

When everyone had gathered around, Pastor Owens prayed over the meal, then the free-for-all began. For dessert, you could hear the motors and ice-grind of the ice cream churns and hear the thick green rinds of the watermelons being cut and cracked open to yield their sweet red meat. A couple hundred chairs had been brought outside but some people had blankets to sit on. Claire helped the boys with their plates and once they were settled down eating, she went back through the line. Karl, Jeb and Marla had already been through. The pastor had already come by to introduce himself.

"Claire, I like the preacher. He seems like a nice man," Marla said.

"You can see the church growing under his pastorship," Karl said.

"Did you like his sermon, Jeb?" Claire asked.

"It was okay. He didn't scream and shout like some of them do."

"He has more of a story-telling style," Claire said. "That's what he calls it. He says everybody can relate to a good story."

"I think that's true," Marla said. "I know I can."

"I wish Momma and Daddy would come to church with us sometime," Claire said. "They could use it."

"Don't hold your breath, sis," Jeb said. "Hey, I gotta find the men's room."

"I'll go with," Marla said, raising Claire's suspicions. Were they going off to make out like a couple of teenagers?

"You want some ice cream?" Karl asked.

"Sure. Get me some peach if there's any," Claire said. She watched the boys playing on the Big Bird beach towel she had spread out for them. Since Sam's attack, he and Toby had learned a different way to play together. They couldn't wrestle on the sofa all the time, or play army in the yard. Sam had to take it easy because the myasthenia gravis could be stirred up by physical exertion. They played quietly together with their little Transformers and Lord of the Rings figures.

Someone honked their car horn. Claire looked up to see Jeb and Marla driving toward her in the Jeep Wrangler. She stood up as Jeb pulled to a stop and climbed out.

"For you, sis," he said, his arms open wide.

"What do you mean?" Claire asked, trying to comprehend the moment. "A Wrangler? Oh my God!" Claire jumped up and ran into her brother's arms. He knew what a piece of shit the Celica was, he'd done the repairs to keep it running and knew the engine was about to go. He had painted the Wrangler fire engine red and put real lamb's wool covers on the front seats.

"It's for you. Happy birthday, Little Red," Jeb said. She had completely forgotten it was her birthday, she was 26. The church started singing Happy Birthday and when she turned to face them, Jackie Mackie, a woman from their Sunday School class, stepped forward with a huge sheet cake filled with candles. Claire had never been so surprised in all her life. By the time they finished singing, she had started crying, and it took two huffs between tears to blow out all the candles.

"Come on, let's take a spin around the parking lot," Jeb said. "This clutch takes some getting used to." Claire looked at Karl. He had known all along. He had remembered it was her birthday and helped set up the surprise. His smile warmed her heart, and all the loving attention from the church made her feel even more loved and accepted. It was like Jesus' love was flowing out through them. It was one of the best feelings she'd ever known.

Aisha

In the gravel lot at Nicholas Park, Claire and Marla warmed their thighs on the hood of Tommy's Chevelle SS, and it was a testament to his equally warm feelings for Marla that he allowed them to lounge there, or was it because they made nice hood ornaments perched as they were like playmates on his canary yellow paint job? They could easily have graced a grease monkey's calendar.

From where she sat, Claire could barely see the speck of her husband standing in left field for American Can where he was listening to the hum of metal halide lights. The ballasts made a droning sound that got inside his head the way a skeeter gets in your ear. To Karl, not making a stupid mistake was the crucial thing. Left field made him a little crazy. He was boxed in by the night, by the darkness behind him and above, where once in a while the ball would appear, a white dot arcing toward him. It was then, when his eyes locked on the ball and his body began to maneuver, as everyone watched, that he had a chance at glory.

All his buddies from the can factory were there. Working as a kitter had been the best job he'd ever landed. Not that the work of a kitter was so fulfilling, it was the fringe benefits that made the job meaningful, the cheap six-packs of beer and energy drinks available to every employee. American Can was a private label can maker and custom brewer.

It was what they called a vertical operation, everything was under one roof, and all the technology was state-of-the-art. The can-making operation was separate from the brewery, the two sections of the plant were connected by a ground-level walkway, and an overhead conveyor carried the pristine, newly minted cans into the area they called the "filling station." Karl had worked in the brewery warehouse at the other end of the vast facility (largest employer in Sampson County). His job was to collect the ingredients required for a batch of beer or soft drinks, stack the sacks of sucrose and flavorings on a wooden pallet and forklift them into the brewery, where they were dumped into vats. These guys surrounding him in the cool evening air, smacking their fists into well-used gloves, spitting juice from their chaws and dips, were his asshole buddies, his brave comrades in the battle against small town boredom and insanity, basically his drinking crew. Even though he was employed by Walmart now, they still wanted him in left field.

During the seventh inning, the Indians started to arrive with their Dodge Rams and trailers filled with tables and tarps and began setting up on the fair grounds adjacent to the softball field. Every time another vehicle pulled in, its headlights flashed across the outfield. When a batter for Southern Power popped the ball high into left field and Karl drifted over to get under it, a teenage hoop dancer shone his low beams directly into Karl's eyes, accidently, of course, and this caused him to lose sight of the ball, which plummeted downward and struck his shoulder, creating an awful, searing pain through muscle and collar bone. He gasped and dropped to his knees, his glove slipped from his limp left hand, then, with slow-motion drama, his face sillyputtied into a Munchesque shape, and he fell sideways, like a defeated king on a chess board, into the dew-laden grass. He lay still for some time, twenty seconds or so, and his fellow fielders ran over to look at him. One of them gave a thumbs up to assure the onlookers that their left fielder wasn't dead or fatally injured.

Claire thought seriously about running out there.

"You're not going to run out there?" Marla asked.

"You think I should?" Then she realized that some of the women who knew her and Karl were watching her to see how she was going to respond. It was a public test of their marriage. Claire hopped off the hood and walked through the parking lot. When she got to the American Can dugout, Mike Whistler, a guy she'd known since elementary school, swung open the gate and she strode onto the field with a rising sense of purpose. Now she knew how Marla felt when she was in homecoming court. Two players from American Can had walked to the fence and were yelling at the Indians to stop shining their lights into the game. They were yelling at no one in particular. The young man who had blinded Karl for that fateful moment was talking to his friends, oblivious to the softball game. Claire remembered lacrosse games played at night in damp, freshly mowed grass. She missed running until her lungs ached and sweating like a race horse. As she crossed the infield, Karl sat up and people began to clap, and she thought they might be clapping because she was marching out there, but it never dawned on her that, while some people thought it was a sweet gesture, most of the men were thinking what a pussy Karl was. Hell, this was *softball*. And it had hit him in the *shoulder*. By the time Claire got out to left field, Karl was back on his feet. He glared at her the way husbands glare at their wives, looking murderous.

"What do you think you're doing?" he said angrily.

"You alright?" Claire asked, but now she could care less.

"Yeah, I'm fine," he said, then he moved his arm in a circular motion and winced. "I'll have a bruise is all," he groaned.

"Well, I'm going out with Marla, so you have to pick up the boys. Since you don't drink anymore." She turned and walked away without getting an answer.

She and Marla walked over to look at what the Croatans were doing. The annual tribal pow-wow was the next day. Hundreds of Native Americans would flood into Newton Grove to take part in the festival of Indian culture. The folks who had come out tonight were setting up the craft tables and tents. Park employees had already set up bleachers around the stomp dance area and some young men were building the Grandfather fire in the center. A car drove past her and Marla, the same Camaro she'd seen at the Inferno, the Camaro that belonged to Storm Eagle. He was pulling a trailer imprinted with Gator Creek Taxidermy on the side. He parked and Claire and Marla walked over. He didn't seem surprised to see them standing next to his car when he got out. Claire wondered if he thought she was cute. She was wearing a snug-fitting knit top and tight jeans, and she tried to look at him in a sexy way through the smoke of the cigarette between her lips. She dropped it on the ground and crushed it under a sandal, his eyes tilted down and she was glad she'd painted her toenails pink. He stepped toward them, then passed them, a small, curious smile on his face. Claire saw his scarred, mud-encrusted boots. He was probably a hunter, too. Maybe worked lumber. Or maybe he'd been out on another search and rescue. They watched him open the trailer. Inside were shelves holding all kinds of preserved animals – a fox, raccoon, skunk, hawk, and fish mounted on plaques. He pulled out a folding table like they use in church fellowship halls.

"You need some help?" Claire chirped.

"Not really," he said, walking by without looking back. They followed him and watched him set up the table. "Can I help you ladies with something?" he asked. He pushed a steel table leg into place and looked up.

"Did you stuff all them animals?" Claire asked.

"That's what I do. I'm a taxidermist."

"They look so real," Marla said. "You do good work."

"Thank you," he said. "I try to capture the spirit of the animal."

"That can't be easy, capturing a spirit," Claire said. He looked at her like she'd said something important, thought-provoking. She'd surprised him, but he wasn't sure he wanted to talk to her. He'd just had a stupid argument with his girlfriend and it was tempting to use these two as balm. He'd dated a white girl before and knew they could be fun, and silly in a way Indian girls were not.

"How do you know animals even have spirits?" Marla

asked, trying to prod him.

"Everything has a spirit," he said in a sure tone that settled the matter. He walked back to the trailer and removed some folding chairs. Claire stared at a huge, slick-furred beaver that was staring down at her from its shelf.

"That beaver ... wow," Claire said.

She and Marla each took a chair and he carried two.

"Does your friend have a name?" he asked.

"This is Marla. Marla, this is Storm Eagle." Claire imagined an eagle flying through lightning and rain, hunting rabbits and other rodents, using its keen vision and deadly talons.

"Indians have cool names, don't they," Claire said. She knew she sounded stupid but it was too late. She wasn't happy with the way Marla was looking at Storm Eagle, flirting with that practiced smile of hers, biting her lip while she checked him out. Marla was used to picking up guys and better at it than Claire was.

"Storm Eagle sure is a great Indian name," Marla said.

"Thank you," Storm Eagle said.

"If I were an Indian what would be a good name for me?" Marla asked.

"How would I know?" Storm Eagle said.

"I mean, what would you name me if you had to?"

"Little Fox, maybe," Storm Eagle said, smiling.

"Or how about, "Big Running Mouth," Claire said.

"Funny," Marla said, wanting to punch Claire in the nose.

"Storm Eagle is the one who found that lost girl I told you about," Claire said.

"That was you, huh? Wow." Marsha sounded very impressed.

"Yes, that was me. And my brothers."

"The sign cutters," Claire said.

"That's right. How's that little girl doing?" he asked.

"Fine, far as I know," Claire said.

"Good," Storm Eagle said. "I worry about that little one."

He positioned the table and chairs where he wanted them and returned to the trailer. He was inside the trailer when the floodlights went out. Until their irises adjusted, they were sealed in darkness. Claire went to the chain link fence and saw someone carrying a cake into the American Can dugout. It was somebody's birthday. The game had ended and the Southern Power boys were getting into their pickups. Two American Can players carried a washtub filled with ice and beer into the dugout. Claire wondered if Karl would drink a beer. Somebody blew out the cake candles and then somebody turned the lights back on. As they reset, you could hear electricity sizzling in the filaments. The lights blinked then began to glow. Now she could see Karl. He had a beer in his hand. He raised it and drank. She saw J.C.'s souped up Camry enter the parking lot. Tommy was with him. They had gone somewhere to score some weed and blotter (Tommy had to have some blotter).

"Tommy's back," Claire said, then she looked at Storm Eagle. He was watching the birthday celebration and she realized that the white man's world was not his world. He operated in the Indian world and would never work for

American Can or Southern Power, not if he could help it. He probably wondered what it was like over there in the dugout, but he probably didn't care about being one of them. Indians have a way of being who they are born to be. They have their own Great Spirit to talk to.

"We're going to the Inferno. You wanna come?" Claire asked. His eyes met hers, he thought she had a delicate childlike face. He grinned, mulling over the possibilities.

"I have to get home," he said with a hint of regret.

"Maybe we'll come by tomorrow," Marla said. "To see your pow-wow."

"You should do that," he said. "I'll keep an eye out."

Tyler Elkin was having a very, very, very good day. He had made love to his new girlfriend that morning, wrote 2,000 words on a novel he was desperately eager to finish, and had just read an email from the provost of Barstow College saying they wanted him to join their faculty for the spring semester. No more community college classes with nursing students and paralegals wasting their time, and his, vainly trying to make literature. Everyone writes, he often told his students, everyone can write something, but that's not what makes you an author of novels or short stories or poetry. Real literature requires a sophistication of thought and language and imagination that only gifted people are able to achieve.

"This gift," he told his class that afternoon, "is rare, like pearls. You can pry open a hundred oysters but only one in a million will hold a pearl of real value. I mean a perfect, natural pearl, a natural writer." He walked around to the front of his desk. "I can show you how to create a cultured pearl, but the perfect natural pearl is a phenomenon."

Tyler was at least six one, and might have appeared lanky except that he worked out with free weights and his chest and shoulders were ripped, his waist narrow and tight. Claire thought he had the lean, muscular physique of a swimmer, and his skin was smooth and tanned, definitely more tanned than you would expect on a community college writing teacher. His eyes were set beneath a Roman brow that made him seem intelligent and thoughtful, and the color of his eyes reminded Claire of Wild Turkey bourbon. Big Eddie treated himself to a new fifth every Thanksgiving, made it last until Christmas, and would pour a finger into a clear glass, undiluted, under his Famous Faces of NASCAR lamp where light swirled in it like liquid amber. That was the color of Elkin's eyes. Those eyes smiled at you, those eyes made you feel warm, and could make a woman feel drunk. Claire sat there admiring the poetry of Elkin's eyes and the muscles in his arms, and immersed herself in his voice as he talked about Thoreau and Whitman, and Galway Kinnell and John Logan, as he read to them like a father bewitching his children at bedtime, creating, not an academic experience, but, for the females in the room, a shared erotic dreamstate.

Claire wasn't sure what this poetry business was all about. Tyler seemed nice enough, but he took writing so seriously. Claire wasn't sure she would fit in. She'd only written one poem in her whole life, that she could remember. It was about a frog in a pond that refused to leave its lily pad. She wrote it in the ninth grade. Some of the girls in Tyler's class looked smart, some were hippies, a few were just poor, dumb country girls. One girl looked part Croatan and there was one Mexican guy named Hector, a short, handsome kid with a shock of black hair.

"We are going to write twenty poems in this class and we are going to read at least a hundred poems, we are going to analyze poems, and you are going to memorize a poem and recite it for the class, all in an attempt to become more intimate with poetic techniques and language. If you have a problem with any of this, please drop the class today." Claire raised her hand, Tyler pointed at her.

"What if the last poem you wrote was in the ninth grade?"

"Then you are probably in the right place. This is Sampson County's springboard to literary virtuosity and, in fact, the only writing class of any kind, other than my short story class, in the whole county. Just because you've only written one poem in your entire life doesn't mean you aren't a natural pearl, it just means you have no passion for writing, and, since passion means everything when it comes to being a writer, I suggest you try to get yourself some."

After class, a girl approached Claire. She wore a wrap-around skirt and tank top without a bra, soft brown under arm hair poking out like corn silk. Claire got a faint whiff of body odor and patchouli.

"My name is Aisha," she said, extending her hand. Silver bangles jangled on her wrist.

"Claire McGill."

"I want to start a poetry group. Would you like to be in it?"

"What do you do exactly, in a group like that?"

"I haven't started it yet, I'm just looking for some people, maybe four in all. We can read our poems and try to make them better, but there's rules, I found them online at Writer's Café. It'll be fun. We'll try not to be too cruel."

"Well that's good."

"So you want to do it?" Aisha tilted her head slightly. Aisha was not the kind of girl Claire would normally talk to or hang out with, but she had a breezy, natural sophistication and earthy sweetness that Claire admired.

"Sure, I'll come. Just let me know when and where. I've got two boys, so I'll have to get Karl or Momma to watch them."

"You've got two boys, no way, you're not old enough to have children."

"It don't take special talent to make babies," Claire said.

"Yeah, I guess not. Do you want to get some lunch?" Aisha tilted her head again to underscore the question.

They drove to a place Claire had never been to before. It was called Taqueria, a Mexican place. Usually if she felt like Mexican, she went to Taco Bell in Clinton, but this place was run by Mexicans and it was in a house with a big front porch they had painted in the brightest colors imaginable. They ordered Coronas. Aisha helped Claire order. There wasn't a menu and everybody spoke Mexican.

"How did you learn to speak Mexican?" Claire asked.

"You mean Spanish? I worked on a farm with a bunch

of migrant laborers, mostly Spanish-speaking. But I also took Spanish in high school." Aisha took a long swig from her Corona.

"You speak it real good," Claire said.

"Thanks. You know, I'm surprised you weren't pissed at what Tyler said. He's such a smartass."

"You mean about finding some passion?" Claire dipped a tortilla chip into the bowl of salsa fresca.

"Yeah, I thought he insulted you."

"True is true, I guess. I don't know why I even signed up for the course."

"You're amazing," Aisha said scooping up a load of salsa, popping it into her mouth.

"I don't think I'm amazing at all. Why would you say that?"

"You're a rebel, Claire. You refuse to accept the status quo of Hicksville."

"This really is Hicksville, isn't it." The waitress in her colorful skirt returned with their plates of steaming food.

"This is the hickest down I've ever lived in, and I don't even think "hickest" is a word but it sure as hell applies. And you're doing your own thing even though you've got two kids. That's fucking amazing. Power on, girl."

"I probably should be picking them up right now."

"Who, your kids? Where are they? Daycare?"

"No, they've never been in daycare. I can't afford it. Momma keeps them."

"It's good she'll do that. My mother would never do that."

"Why not?"

"She hates me, so she'd probably hate my children." Aisha said it like she didn't care, or had accepted it and there was no patching things up. When Claire and J.J. had an argument they always made up the very next day.

"Why does she hate you?" Claire asked, rubbing the cool mouth of the beer bottle against her lips.

"Maybe because I ran away when I was sixteen and didn't call for two years."

"Where'd you go?"

"All over. San Diego. Phoenix. Then back south again to Charleston, spent three years there, waitressing, you know, and going to school. Then finally up here to Newton Grove."

"Why'd you come here? To Hicksville?"

"I read Tyler's novel, *This Side of Somewhere Else*, and I decided I wanted to study with him, even if it was at a community college. Tyler is a bona fide genius of the contemp lit scene, in my opinion he's up there with David Foster Wallace, and god, I love Wallace, too." The Mexican waiter returned to refill their water glasses.

"Where are you from? I mean, before you ran away?" Claire asked.

"Delaware."

"Delaware? I don't even know where that is."

"It hardly matters. Hey, I want to meet your mother sometime."

"You're kidding. Why on earth would you want to do that?"

"I'd like to see how a real mother and daughter get along."

A week later, Claire invited Aisha to lunch at her parents' house. J.J. had made a tuna casserole, yeast rolls, sliced tomatoes and a fresh pitcher of sweet tea. Big Eddie was watching TV in the room adjacent to the kitchen. For some reason, J.J. had not prepared him for their visit. He hadn't shaved and he was wearing a soiled wife-beater.

Tomatoes and rolls were all Aisha ate. She didn't intend to offend J.J., she just believed it was horrible what the fishermen did to tuna. Their fishing techniques were tortuous, she told Claire later. But that wasn't the worst of the visit.

"Don't you shave your underpits, dear?" J.J. asked.

"No ma'am," Aisha said with a nice southern drawl.

"Why not?" J.J. snapped back, sensing the pepper in Aisha's reply.

"I don't like to use deodorant. It contains aluminum dioxide you know."

"Are you a vegetarian?"

"No ma'am. It's just the tuna. They have rights, too."

"They do? Like what?"

"Like a right to stay alive in the ocean."

" Momma, shut up, you're embarrassing her," Claire said.

"No, really, it's okay. I think its funny," Aisha said.

"See, Momma, she thinks you're funny."

"I didn't say that," Aisha said. She looked at J.J. for a reaction.

"I've just never in my life seen anything so ... so rude," J.J. said.

"Rude? I'm sorry if I was rude," Aisha said.

"In the south it's only polite to eat what's put in front of you. There's some poor folks who don't have it so good, and a tuna casserole would mean something to them."

" Momma, you are acting so Hicksville!" Claire said, "and Daddy in that damn wife-beater, I swear. He looks like the biggest redneck."

"We are rednecks I guess," J.J. said, "but at least we use proper hygiene." Aisha was not going to be sucked into this fuss even though she was the focus of it, at least she wasn't going to articulate what she was thinking about Claire's parents. She had hoped that meeting J.J. might unlock the secrets of her heart, the secret to why she and her mother could not abide each other. But it only made her grieve for Claire. Aisha's mother was college educated and ten times as sophisticated in her tastes, but no different than J.J. in her compulsion to buy meaningless crap to adorn her meaningless life. That's how Aisha saw it, anyway. And now, through the accident of birth and the new intentional life she had discovered, Claire was seeing her mother with new eyes. She was seeing her mother's small-mindedness, and her limitations. It made Claire angry. Why did she have to grow up in such a home? With two bona fide rednecks. Why did her parents have to be an anchor in her life instead of a sail? A lot of who she was all their fault.

The poetry group met at a coffee shop called Mugg's in Clinton. It had formerly been a dime store called Jep's Five n' Dime that had been operating since the 1920s. The third generation owner had converted it to a barrel candy store, along with toys and gifts, local Croatan crafts, lawn furniture, garden supplies and a hodgepodge of other merchandise. Eventually Walmart put it out of business. But hell, Walmart had sucker-punched downtown Clinton's simple economy and left half the storefronts empty and available to Latino churches and Montagnard nail salons.

The owners of Mugg's bought a used $2,000 espresso machine, a wireless system, and fanciful cafe tables and chairs: overnight it became one of the hottest little joints in the county.

The girls, Aisha, Claire and Livia, sat at a table in the corner. Livia had ordered a coffee drink that looked like it had marshmallow on top.

"What's that?" Claire asked.

"It's a cappuccino. Try it. I have to put sugar in mine." Claire sipped the drink. It tasted like coffee to her. Livia was one of those smart girls who disguises herself with a stylish haircut and hip clothes.

Ember was last to arrive. She was a Croatan mixed with other bloodlines (some Caucasian, some Hispanic and/or African) and in her case the chemistry had not yielded another Angelina Jolie. Ember carried extra weight and football-size breasts.

"I used to date him," Livia said, indicating the young man behind the counter. Claire thought he was cute.

"What happened?" Claire asked.

"He got so possessive I couldn't breathe."

Ember was nursing a first-class inferiority complex: "I'd let him possess me," she said. "Bless my soul."

"Let's don't talk about men, let's talk about poetry," Aisha said. "That's why we're here, right?"

"I've never done this before," Claire said.

"What do you want to talk about?" Livia asked.

"Maybe we should read a poem and talk about it," Ember suggested.

"Maybe they have something here," Aisha said.

She walked over to a bookshelf that held a stack of board games and a short row of books.

"Either Rod McKuen, *Listen to the Warm*, or Emily Dickinson. I say Emily Dickinson." She handed a paperback collection of Dickinson's poems to Livia. "Here, you read us something, Livia." Livia thumbed through the book. "Why don't you just read *This is my letter to the world*," Aisha said.

Livia read ...

> **"This is my letter to the world,**
> **That never wrote to me,–**
> **The simple news that Nature told,**
> **With tender majesty.**
> **Her message is committed**
> **To hands I cannot see;**
> **For love of her, sweet countrymen,**
> **Judge tenderly of me!"**

"So, what do you think of it?" Aisha asked.

"I like it," Claire said. "It's pretty."

"You've got to go a little deeper than that, Claire," Aisha said.

"She's saying that her poetry is about nature," Livia said. "But what does it mean when she says, 'Her message is committed to hands I cannot see'? If it was committed to her hands, she could see them."

"Maybe she means God's hands," Ember said.

"If it was God's hands, obviously you couldn't see them," Livia said. "So why would she even write that?"

"Maybe the message is in her hands," Claire said. "But maybe it's a mystery to her."

"That's good, Claire. I think you might be right," Aisha said. "How ironic, we're here to talk about being writers of poetry, and our first poem is about Emily's 'letter to the world,' her poetry."

Claire took the book from Livia.

"You know what I like?" Claire said, "It's when she says the world never wrote to her. It makes you feel sad for her."

"Why do you like that?" Livia asked.

"I don't know. It's like the kid who writes to a pen pal who never writes back. Why can't the world take the time to write back?"

"But that's all metaphorical," Aisha said. "She doesn't expect the world to write back."

"What's it a metaphor for?" Ember asked.

"What's a *metaphor?*" Claire asked. Aisha glanced at Livia in disbelief.

"A metaphor is a comparison. It's when you describe one thing in terms of another thing," Livia explained.

"Linguists say that virtually all language relies on metaphor," Aisha added.

"Like 'hot as hell' is a metaphor," Livia said, "or 'dumb as a rock.'"

"Oh. I see," Claire said. "That's cool."

"'Cool' is also a metaphor," Aisha said.

Livia continued: "So, in this poem, 'writing a letter to the world' means she is speaking through poetry to whoever will listen. It doesn't mean she is actually writing a letter."

"'The news that nature told' is another metaphor, right?" Ember asked.

"Right," Aisha said. "Emily Dickinson was one of the most modern poets in her day. One of the reasons was her use of original metaphors. I'm glad we're starting with her poetry. She lived a very lonely life, though, a really secluded life."

"She lived alone?" Claire asked.

"She lived in the countryside near Amherst, Massachusetts, and she hardly ever left the house, she always wore white, and she hardly ever had visitors," Aisha said.

"Her poetry wasn't even published, except for a few pieces, until after she died," Livia said. "Look at her picture." Livia held up the book, on the back cover was a picture of Emily. "Look how young she is. This is the only photograph of her, from when she was a teenager."

"How do you two know so much about her?" Ember

asked.

"We took an American literature course last semester," Aisha said.

"Tyler taught it," Livia said, it was awesome. *He* is awesome. Have you read it, *This Side of Somewhere Else?* It's just an awesome freakin' read."

"You sound like you're in love with him," Claire said.

"I am in love with him, but just in a soul sense, I'd never sleep with him," Aisha said. "That would ruin everything."

"Well that's good, I guess," Ember said. "I'd probably sleep with him but I really don't see myself getting the chance."

A Mind on Fire

Twelve Poems

by

Claire McGill

In the Springtime of 2011, my friend Aisha Moore and my Sampson County College professor Tyler Elkin who wrote the awesome novel *This Side of Somewhere Else* helped me fix up twelve poems from my class writing assignments in "Beginner Poetry: Finding a Voice" to get published by the college English Dept. In the writing of these poems I bared my soul as best I could and bent language to do my will since I'm told that is what poetry is supposed to do.

I hope you like them.
Thanks, Claire McGill

A Mind on Fire

Momma loves Big Lots
discounts and wide variety
and when I said she didn't need
another yard gnome, she implied
I was dumb, but she's the one
who quit high school
when she was only fifteen
that's what I was thinking
when my mind was trying
to shut down in high school.
I knew my destiny was cast
because I'm a singlewide girl
but I got a doublewide mind
and words pour out my mouth
like a flamethrower burning up
my old redneck life now
and Momma's wondering
who I done become to say
"Big Lots sucks, Momma,
all this cheap crap in here."
And she starts to cry
because she believes
more in cheap crap
than in Jesus his own self.
And in the sunlight outside
my mind caught fire again
and through my life in flames
my eyes can see Momma
just is doing what she can
with what Big Lots sells her
and what life gave her.

The Wrangler

He comes up like Dracula
out of his grave, a wrench
in his black grease hand
up from under there checking out
a Jeep Wrangler that looks like
its embarrassed with its wheels
off like that and dirty belly showing
and axles and springs and brakes.
That's my brother Jeb I say
to myself, wondering about him
the way he's always stuck under cars
all day and only a black and white
tv in the corner with the picture
rolling up every five seconds
bouncing and rolling over
and over like life does, like days
always the same life one second
after the other, and no color
and no sound, just cicadas
in August, hot as dishwater
Jeb sweating like a hog in season
and me too, so its Cheerwine time
I say and get him one and me too.
And its good, Coke and cherry
together like that in one bottle
like me and him at that minute
cold thirst quenchers tilted up
and drinking them together.

Crystal Things

What love I have of crystal things
and the shininess of them
and see-throughness of them
like icicle daggers in wintertime
and cubes in a glass of tea
frosted up window panes
crackling across its surface
with millions of crystals
and all them millions of
tiny ice particles, every one
trying their best to reflect
my face, like they would love
to hold me, maybe know me
and have me in there with them
and that's how all reflections
are, like the Croatan Indians
say a picture steals the soul
I think crystal things steal
my soul and makes me clear.

Barbie's Clarinet

If Barbie played the clarinet
would God be listening to her I ask.
Does he listen to me?
Or Emily D. or Aisha, us women
who never can be Barbies.
But we feel like plastic
sometimes, I do
and I wanted a clarinet
always, always wanted one
but they were all given out
in band at my old high school
that was made of quarry stone.
But when you sing
in the quarry where the stone
was cut out by grizzly men
on huge yellow bulldozers
years before I was born
the echo makes you feel more
than a human being feels.
Like a god with a big voice
him talking to his own self
but not Barbie, only a woman
who got no damn business
driving around a yellow dozer
and no clarinet for her lips
to blow music on.

Man's World

They go round, round again
and again and again, roaring
and if you are like me you got to
cover your ears with your palms
or stick cotton in there.
What does it sound like?
Like a monster, a dragon beast
fifty cars flashing by I'll bet
when the stupid thing gets started
all together one gigantic roar
like all the energy of all the men
in the whole world's countries
who make and race them cars
them shiny fucking Nascar cars
and drink all that Pabst Blue Ribbon
and beat up their wives and girlfriends
back home or right in the parking lot.
And yes I have fury, cause I been there.
I been beat up and been to Winston Cup.
And it's all a man's world like I said
nothing but a man's fucked up world
and nothing for a girl to do but grin
like she's stupid like I did and deal
and buy herself a gun maybe
and use it if she's got to
since that's what it's made for.
I don't mean killing her husband
but maybe her own self
or maybe just shooting at a stump
or Spaghetti Os can
putting a hundred holes in it
like she's got in her head
probably anyway for marrying
a man who loves cars better
than his own pretty wife.

In a Singlewide

Much can happen in a singlewide
right here in the musty air between
aluminum walls is where I live
with all the boys I love, and maybe
maybe, maybe even my husband
Karl, a Walmart man now
and growing more responsible.
A singlewide is a home
and people live in 'em just like
me, I live here in my singlewide, but
I live bigger inside my mind.
I am human, and I am young
and all my dreams want to bust
out of these sad aluminum walls
and explode into the sky like I was
a big rocket from South of the Border
and I will explode it my own self
because this is my above the earth tomb
a tomb made out of aluminum
in a factory of happy men with jobs
making decent metal homes for the poor
who can't afford no better but know
a lot worse until a tornado rips it
right up, up into the air one night.
The poor just gotta live with danger
and god don't I know that's true.
'Cause right here on this shag carpet
my husband beat me black and blue.
But am I dead yet, no I am not
not, not dead yet, as you can see
by these here words coming
out from a mind on fire
like storm lightning flashing
from a black mountain of clouds
or gasoline on an old bald tire.

Cherry

It's okay to say the eff word
my professor Tyler said
to the whole class today
and then he said go
make a poem about someone
so here goes – Cherry
I hope it's okay to use
your name since you're in the hospital
and maybe insane, and coming off
the meth and hating yourself
about the abortion you had.
I think about you a lot
and how fucked up you are.
There, I used it, how you like that
Tyler, the professor, I know
you are really a lecturer
and never got your masters
but I'm gonna read your novel
one day, *This Side of Somewhere Else*
cause its wonderful everybody says
and I'll give it to Cherry the girl
who is red inside and red outside
like her name says, red the color
of hurting, stopping, and anger.
How fucked up you are Cherry
and maybe not too insane
not anymore than me
or the whole world is.

Metaphors

I am just a metaphor
for myself, I am like I am
cause I was made country
but that ain't all I'm stuck with.
Maybe I can make more metaphors
like I am Claire the poetess, I am
Claire the movie star, Claire
the Indian Princess, Claire
made of crystals and snowflakes
(that never ever melt)
and Claire the sunshine
Claire the rainbow
Claire the love goddess
Claire the school student
(and SCC graduate one day)
Claire the girl who escaped
her aluminum prison
and made a good metaphor
out of herself.

Jesus is Big

Jesus is big, big, big
bigger than the universe
the biggest love there is
big, big, big, he deserves
the best colors and guitars
and decorations and singers.
Preachers preach about him
about all he said in the Holy Word
and did, how he died for your sins
and mine too but my sins
are what has stained my soul
like brown rust streaks
on our singlewide home.
Nobody knows a girl's sins
like the girl her own self
knows herself and her sinning.
Nobody knows the evil
deep down in me, and
know one knows the inside
where the tears come up
from and the poetry.

Sweet Tea

Drinking it cold
is the best thing
ever on a hot day
from hell itself, days
like this is what God
gave us sweet tea for
in green glasses with ice
crystals chilling it down
and I wash down barbecue
and tomato sandwiches
and Lays potato chips
with it, and more, everything
all the food in the world and
all the miseries in the world
wash down good enough
with sweet tea, sweet tea
good cold sweet tea.
I love it to death
and it loves me.

The World Is Cruel

On the news it looks like
everything is upside down
and inside out, lots of wars
and earthquakes like endtimes
or something like God's wrath
pouring out like fire on us
but not me where I live, me
and mine we got it okay
by comparison I mean.
Call us trailer trash
or stupid rednecks
I really don't care, I mean
the world is being tore apart
like I don't know what.
At least I got my two boys
and at least they can read
and do math pretty good
cause its gonna be a hard
hard world for them.
They still gotta grow up
and deal with all that.
But today's world is cruel.
Today's world is fucked up.
Nobody's giving no guarantees
not that I can see, no promises
and there's a ton of debt in America
like they talk about on the news.
I know my boys will have to pay
for all that politician greed
and my boys will need jobs
to pay it with or buy fishing worms
even or catfish dough or whatever.
It's that kind of world today. Cruel.
No money, no worms, no fishing.
Or it will be soon, when our kids
get grown and me and you
are just old wrinkled shucks
of human beings.

Freight Train

He was a loved man once
when he was young and we
did it everywhere like we
could not get enough of each
other and that feeling filled us up
on sweaty flesh, pot and cold beer
and that was all we cared about.
But now Karl my husband
is a shiftless man, that word
is what Daddy called him
and Daddy and my brother Jeb
work hard so they know.
But I am honored and proud
of Karl's Tire n' Lube job
because he's working hard
changing and selling tires
and oil and brake jobs
bringing home benefits
and being part of something
bigger than him or us:
the Walmart family.
But in me, deep down
there's a restless girl
and she wants more than sex
and Pabst and maryjane.
She wants more than a man
can give her, or motherhood.

She wants a lot more!

Even Jesus who is big
and wonderful as all get out
can't give her what she wants.
She wants more than you Karl
and it hurts to write it down
or think it in her brain
or feel it or say it out loud
right to your face since you
and her and them two sweet boys
are one unit about to be broken
into a million pieces of sad
because divorce is coming down
down on you and her like a sledge
or freight train shaking the earth.
The freight train of the future
carrying all that weight
loaded up from the past
hurtin' each other like that
surely Karl we gotta knowed
it was gonna be a bad crash.

Cherry

Applebees was as busy as usual on Sunday, but Jeb and Karl had grabbed a corner table they could all fit around. Claire slipped into the booth beside Big Eddie, he slipped his arm around her shoulders, her damp hair was cold and tickled his arm, the silky orange hairs on his arm tickled her neck. She wondered what he thought of their church. He never talked about God and wasn't about to join the Tabernacle, even though he'd seen a lot of friends at the morning service, guys who used to waste afternoons at the garage. Karl had delayed his baptism until Claire was ready to be immersed with him. Claire knew from the look in Big Eddie's eyes how pleased he was with her. He had already announced he was going to pick up the check, and he and J.J. were living off their paltry 401Ks.

Marla and Jeb were almost like a dating couple. That happens when a guy and girl are the only singles among the married, suddenly they have to band together, at least until after the turtle fudge pie, but for Marla and Jeb coupling was easy, an old habit, as comfortable as a faded T-shirt. Jeb had cleaned up real nice. Shaved and cologned, he'd surprised them all. He'd given Claire a big hug when she and Karl came back to the sanctuary after getting baptized. She had no idea Jeb was so strong, his chest and arms so thickly muscled. Somehow she thought of him as the allergy-stricken little brother she could wantonly abuse. Marla had given her a hug, too, and J.J.

and Big Eddie, and the boys. She would be feeling all loved up and warm if it weren't for what she saw Jackie Mackie do. They were getting ready to be baptized. Jackie was one of the baptizees, too. They'd put on shorts and T-shirts in the men's and women's bathrooms and were lining up to go down into the baptismal pool. That's when she saw Jackie, the divorcee from their Sunday School class, the forty-one-year-old Christian cougar who worked at the 24-Hour Diner, eyeing Karl, stealing a lascivious glance at him when nobody else was looking, nobody but his wife, that is, and it could have been more than a glance, it could have been a flirt, because Claire could not see if Karl returned the flirt or not, it had happened so quickly, just as the wide lavender curtain was opening, revealing them to the congregation like contestants in a game show. Claire's heart fluttered when she saw the blue baptismal waters in the pool below them, reminding her of the time she jumped off the second story railing of the Uptowner Motel in Clinton into the swimming pool, drunk as a skunk. That night, as she stood on the railing, she didn't think about hitting the concrete floor of the pool and possibly breaking her neck, or about her bra coming off at impact (which it did), she was mesmerized by the light swirling in the water, a liquid evanescent blue, and how the dangerous thrill rose in her chest making her feel like taking the leap was her inevitable destiny – it was the same feeling she got that day she met with Pastor Owens and the rightness and eternality of God's love had dawned on her and she knew she had to accept the cross.

A video camera was perched overhead to show their

scrunched-up faces bigger than life on two gigantic screens when they went under. When Jackie Mackie came out of the water, her nipples were gumdrop-size under her taut T-shirt, since she had decided not to wear a bra, thinking she was at a wet T-shirt contest instead of a pentacostal church where poked-out nipples were frowned upon. But in spite of all that, Claire enjoyed herself. She had grown to love the people of the Tabernacle and wasn't about to let Jackie Mackie spoil her baptism. Pastor Owens had taught her that baptism symbolized new birth, like how a baby in the womb struggles out and bursts free into the air and light, and baptism was also like getting washed. If the dirt of Claire's sins had actually dripped off her, the water would have turned to mud and the drain would have clogged. Claire remembered when her water broke with Sam, drenching her feet and the carpet where she stood in front of the TV, holding the remote, about to flip channels. That was the moment when she grew up, when she knew the baby was coming out and she was going to have to take care of it, when her life flipped to the *Reality Channel.* At the top of the stairs leading down to the baptismal pool, reality hit again. No one knew the deep down her and the deep down secrets she had carried around for so long like stinky laundry. Her new reality was this: Jesus had done his part, now she had to do hers. She could not let HIM down. Even now, sitting under the warmth of her father's arm at Applebees, something was different about her. Her father sensed it. He would never forget the huge TV image of her hair spreading out like fluid flames under the rippling blue water.

They ate and talked for over an hour, and it was nearly perfect, to be saved and eat at Applebees in the same day, nearly perfect, but not quite. Claire had some worries, one was Jackie, but the other was worse, it was the worry that she'd lied to God. She had some secret sins she'd never confessed to anyone. After the baptism she felt clean-slated and connected, but there were still some lingering doubts about whether she'd done it right. There had to be more to it. She would almost have preferred some punishment to go along with the forgiveness. When she was little her father would paddle her with a ping-pong paddle. That always made her feel like her transgressions had been dealt with, especially when he came to her later and hugged her and told he loved her. Jesus dying for her 2000 years ago was maybe a little too easy. For her anyway, not for him.

On the way to the parking lot, Jeb pulled her aside.

"I'm proud of you, sis, finding God and all. Are you surprised I came to church again?"

"Yeah."

"Well, I've got a favor to ask you. Since I been comin' to church with you ..."

"And you gave me a Wrangler."

"Okay, that too." Jeb stopped in his tracks, gripping her elbow. "Will you go visit Cherry? See how she's doin'?"

"You're worried aren't you? I can understand how you'd be worried about her after she tried to kill herself. Sure, I'll go see her. Why not." Though her heart was filled with reluctance, she could do that much for Jeb. She didn't particularly like Cherry, and Cherry didn't particularly like her either, as far as she knew. But she could do this.

Professor Weston was no Indiana Jones, but he was Sampson Community College's closest contender. On outings, he wore a long-bill fly fishing cap with a logo for Florida Guides Association and three handmade flies stuck in it, and he carried an archeologist's satchel that looked like a brown doctor's bag. In it he had a rock hammer, chisels, brushes, plaster, maps, measuring tape, Ziploc baggies and countless other tools for discovering the existence of primitive man.

On Thursday, he led a Native American History caravan to the Croatan lodge just five miles from the college. The lodge was a building made out of logs like something the pioneers or an ambitious Boy Scout troop would have built. The floors were made of thick pine boards. Rustic windows filled the single big room with light, the sills littered with dead flies, wasps and moths. There were stuffed deer heads on the walls and stuffed foxes and beavers and racoons on the shelves, there were Indian artifacts: leatherwork, arrowheads and ax heads, baskets, pottery. All of it quite beautiful and dusty like forgotten treasure.

At the counter where you could pay for postcards and trinkets, there stood an old Indian wearing long grey braids. His eyes were watery with tears that wouldn't fall. He answered their questions in short, thoughtful sentences with long, thoughtful pauses. The photographs fascinated Claire. A wonderful collection of black and whites: Croatan chieftains, families in aboriginal costume, a crowd of children in front of a one-room schoolhouse. She knew the Croatan tribe shared a common history with her grandfather and great grandfather. She wondered if her ancestors had been gracious and understanding toward the native people. Did they share some common blood reaching back to the time when Irish monks landed in North Carolina? The more she learned about the Indians of the Carolinas, the Croatan, Algonquin and Cherokee, the more uncomfortable she was. Why did the guilt seem to fall on her? Wasn't it guilt? Guilt for bringing disease to the continent. Guilt for stealing their land. Guilt for the Trail of Tears, for Wounded Knee? But why did she feel it so acutely, as if their suffering belonged within her, as if their ghosts had been assigned to haunt her.

While the professor was explaining how the Miocene Epoch had left marine fossils in the sandhills, Storm Eagle strode in the front door and the whole class turned to look at him. The old Indian was his father.

"I need to take him home," he said to Professor Weston. "I'll be back in about twenty minutes to lock up."

"They close the lodge at five," the Professor explained to the class.

After some of her colleagues left to get drinks at the convenience store across the street, Claire overheard the professor say to Hector, "That Indian who just came in here is named Storm Eagle, he's one of the best trout men in this county. He'll be the next chief."

"Is that his father?" Claire asked.

"Yes," the professor said, "his name is Shining Owl, he's the Croatan chieftain."

"Are you friends with them?" Claire asked.

"I consider them friends, sure. I was on the reconciliation committee a few years back. You probably don't remember this..." the professor turned to a newspaper article that had been framed and hung on the wall. It was the story of a murder that took place in 1999. "Storm Eagle's brother was shot and killed in a holdup. He was just sixteen years old when those bastards claimed his life. It happened at the store right over there." Claire looked through the cloudy window. The simple little store across the road advertised "Lottery Here," there was an RC Cola sign, and a handpainted board that read, "Blood Worms & Crickets."

"Two caucasian men came in, shot him and left him to die," the Professor said. He stepped up behind her to share the view. "You can still see two bullet holes in the wall if you know where to look for them. All for eighty-seven dollars, that's how much they took. Never did catch the scumsuckers."

"That was Storm Eagle's brother, huh?" Claire asked.

"Yes. His name was Little Wolf."

If you live in Samson County and want Food Stamps (doesn't really matter if you need them or not but if you want them), you go to Sampson County Department of Social Services and talk to the Food Stamps Manager, Ms. Wanda Pitikin. You sit in a smooth fiberglass chair for an hour waiting to be interviewed by Ms. Wanda Pitikin, a large black woman.

Claire was not a racist like her mother and father, she held no anger or better-than-thou feelings in her heart toward African-Americans or Mexican-Americans or Native Americans for that matter, except for large, mean black women, and that was only because of two experiences, one experience in which her father had been beaten up by a black woman at Southern Market when Claire was four years old and they were standing in line at the checkout counter to pay for a six-pack of Old Milwaulkee and a box of marshmallow cookies with coconut on the top, a favorite of four-year-olds. The woman in front of them had a basketful of groceries and they were stuck behind her with their two items. To Claire, a small, skinny thing at four, the woman was mountainous. Just as the checkout girl was finishing, the woman said, "Oh, I forgot something," and proceeded to push past them (she was perhaps 350 lbs., Big Eddie later hypothesized) and smashed her father into the candy display. He held his tongue, and they waited. She had forgotten her Land O' Lakes butter. When she returned with it, her father moved aside rather dramatically, hands in the air as if to avoid touching her. This caught her attention. She laid the butter on the counter and at that moment as the checkout girl was punching the number keys, the cash register ran out of paper. The girl proceeded to change the roll of paper through the tiny side door of the machine, and, at that point, her father uttered the fateful words, "Good God in heaven." The black woman turned to him and said, "What'd you say?"

"I said, 'Good God in heaven,' Big Eddie repeated.

"You gots a problem with me?" she asked.

"No, I don't gots a problem with you, I gots a problem with getting stuck here behind your big fat ass," Big Eddie said. Claire chuckled. The woman shifted her glare from Eddie to her. Claire would forever remember the look in her eyes. It was frightening, as if a demon had been awakened, burst forth and taken control. The woman screamed something and lunged at her father. Her weight and strength were such that he was dragged down, her body on top of his, and while he wanted to punch her in the nose, the size of her arms and fists, with the bulk of her pinning him down, prevented any counterattack. She pummeled him with her fists and slapped him back and forth across the face until the store manager dragged her off. She tried to slap the manager, too, and acted possessed, as if she was intent on killing Claire's father. Claire's emotions had transitioned from absolute amazement to hot fear that her father would be killed, to an adrenal rush of anger. If she had held a gun in her little hand at that moment, she would have aimed it and fired.

The grocery store memory came flooding forward in full color from the historical archive of her brain when she saw Ms. Wanda Pitiken, who was seated at her desk interviewing Food Stamp applicants.

The other large black woman incident happened at Howard Johnson's on her thirteenth birthday. A large black woman was standing at the 28 flavors ice cream counter and Claire, in her youthful enthusiasm, had stepped on the back of her shoe. The woman turned and glared at her with that same quivering anger in her eyes that Claire had witnessed at the grocery store. The woman lectured Claire:

"Walk on your own feet, little girl, not mine. I need

mine for my own self and don't need no little honkey girl what can't keep her feet to herself walking on me."

"She didn't mean to," J.J. replied. J.J. had stepped up behind Claire and proudly placed her hands on her daughter's thin shoulders. J.J.'s resolve and calm impressed Claire.

"Lady, this your little girl?" the woman asked.

"Yes," J.J. said.

"Well you oughta teach her better than to crowd up on people, you oughta teach her better, that's all I'm sayin'," then she glared at Claire again, "What you lookin' at, child, with that nasty face you be givin' me." Claire didn't know what she meant by "nasty face" but it really hurt her feelings. The woman had purchased a huge banana split. She took it from the ice cream boy and turned toward them. It was a two-handed banana split stacked tall, with the vanilla, chocolate and strawberry scoops of ice cream, and the curves of sliced bananas and dripping chocolate syrup and glistening walnuts on display. Two thoughts went through J.J.'s mind at that moment: one, what all that ice cream would look like on the woman's face, and, two, what Big Eddie's face had looked like after the woman at the grocery store had pummeled it. J.J. held her temper, and held on to Claire's shoulders, and they let the woman go without another word. And why? Because she frightened the hell out of them.

Claire sat down in front of Ms. Wanda Pitiken.

"How can I help you?" she asked.

"I'd like to apply for Food Stamps," Claire said.

"I'll need a driver's license, photo I.D., social, birth

record, landlord verification, utility receipt and income records."

"I got most of that with me. My neighbor, Jenn, told me what I needed to bring to show you."

"Well if you don't have it all, you'll need to schedule another interview."

"I think I got it all," Claire said.

"Well most people don't," Ms. Wanda Pitikin said. "Are you married?"

"Yes, my husband's named Karl and we got two boys."

"Well, does he have a job?"

"He is working at Walmart."

"Everybody works at Walmart now. With two kids, you might qualify for stamps. Have you seen our web site?" She handed Claire a brochure. "You can go online and see if you qualify, then we can schedule an interview."

"We don't have a computer," Claire said.

"They have some at the library," Ms. Wanda Pitikin said, "for free."

Claire drove to the Inferno and sat at the bar. There was one biker in there, an old guy with a long grey ponytail who seemed to enjoy oogling her, and Lewis was tending bar. She took her Corona outside to a picnic table under a gigantic Pin Oak. She thought about how ashamed her mother and father would be if she got food stamps. They thought it was like taking charity, they thought McGills should be better than that. But the cost of groceries was going up, up, up, and killing them and they had to find a way to survive. The world was starting to frighten her, almost more than large black women. On the TV there was even a recent story about the end of the world, a man out in California predicting the rapture like in the book of Revelation. Pastor Owens had assured his flock that the rapture man was a nut. "No one knows the day or hour," Pastor Owns said. "But signs of the end are all about us," he also said. Claire didn't want the world to end before she had figured out what to do with her life. She wanted to make her father proud because he had worked so hard to bring her up right, and even though they might be rednecks and she had fucked up everything in her life more than once, well, Sterling had crashed more than once, too, but he kept gettin' it. Did okay for Junior Johnson and even took Daytona in '94 and '95. Claire thought Ms. Wanda Pitikin was nice enough, maybe she even broke the stereotype. She hadn't been mean or called her "nasty face," but in her presence Claire had felt awfully small again. She never wanted to see *Ms. Wanda Pitikin* again. She never wanted to step foot in DSS again, not for any reason, and not for food stamps.

The psychiatric facility in Butner, NC was high security, but Claire had called ahead and gotten permission to visit Cherry. She figured she owed it to Jeb. He had been madly in love with Cherry and said he wanted to marry her, but Cherry was too scary acting at times and Jeb didn't want to marry all her issues. Claire knew how worried and depressed he'd been since Cherry had her brush with the razor blade.

Cherry was polite but standoffish when Claire first arrived in the visiting area. The cuts on her face made her skin look dented and she had one wrist bandaged. She immediately lit a Winston, needing the self-medication provided by nicotine. In Claire's presence, Cherry's mind began racing with thoughts about Jeb, and she blurted out, "I don't even want to live anymore, I really don't. I'm no good for any man. I don't need to be here. When I get out I'm just going to end it. They should save their money." She took a long drag on her cigarette, her fingers twittering nervously. "I tried to kill myself. Couldn't even do that right. I couldn't find the vein and it hurt like hell and I just gave up. I should've used pills or a gun or something that fucking works."

She walked to the window, avoided looking at Claire. "Why the fuck was I ever born, why did God put me on this fucking planet?"

"It's not like anybody asks us if we want to be born," Claire said, perched on the edge of a blue vinyl chair. "We're just here. Shit, in high school you were the most popular girl in the whole school, or one of them."

"Yeah. One of them. But look at me now, my face is all fucked up." The scars made by exploding glass shards were still as raw and pink as bubblegum, and the drugs gave her a blurry look, as if she wasn't quite in focus.

"You can bounce back, can't you, Cherry?"

"You got kids, right, a couple of boys? The only thing I ever loved, I killed."

"What do you mean? What are you talking about?"

"My baby. I killed it. I had an abortion. I thought I had to because they said it would fuck up my life."

"Was it Jeb's baby?" Claire asked. "Was it his?" Cherry nodded her head.

"When I went to the clinic, after they sucked the baby out and I was in the recuperwaiting room, I felt like I had to go to the bathroom..." Cherry looked out the thick-paned window as if telling the story to the glare of sunlight, squinting, as if to see something far away "...and when I got up from the toilet I looked down, and there was blood, and there was a piece of my baby's skull, like a piece of fuckin' egg shell floating in the toilet."

"Oh God, Cherry. That's awful."

"I thought I had to have the abortion. I didn't want to." Cherry was leaning her head so hard against the window pane Claire thought it might break. She put her arm around her. Cherry seemed to have said all she wanted to say. Her shoulders began to heave, like she might throw up, but it was only the convulsions those memories had created and a stream of tears that couldn't wash way the past.

"I'm so sorry, Cherry. But you gotta let that shit go." Claire took her hand. It was cold, the fingers like sticks covered in rubber. She squeezed until Cherry looked at her. "You gotta let go of that and find a way to get well. You hear me?"

"How many ways are there to touch the face of God?" Tyler asked his poetry class the next morning. Ronald

Reagan used that phrase in a speech. He was giving a speech to honor the astronauts who had just died in the Challenger explosion. I think that was around the mid-eighties, right? Before some of you were born. But what most people don't know is that Reagan was quoting a sonnet." Tyler slipped a piece of paper out of his journal. He read:

High Flight

Oh! I have slipped the surly bonds of Earth
And danced the skies on laughter-silvered wings;
Sunward I've climbed and joined the tumbling
mirth of sun-split clouds,
　　　　– and done a hundred things
You have not dreamed of wheeled and soared
and swung
High in the sunlit silence. Hov'ring there,
I've chased the shouting wind along, and flung
My eager craft through footless falls of air...
Up, up the long, delirious, burning blue
I've topped the wind-swept heights with easy grace
Where never lark, or even eagle, flew–
And, while with silent lifting mind I've trod
The high, untrespassed sanctity of space,
Put out my hand and touched the face of God.

Tyler sat on the edge of his desk, "That's the sonnet form. This poem was written during the Second World War by John Gillespie Magee, a pilot with the Royal Canadian Air Force. He was a Spitfire pilot. He was killed in a training flight when he was nineteen." He looked at them to see if he was getting anywhere, making contact with anyone. "Literature has a way of living on, doesn't it? It has a way of outliving us. In *Metamorphoses*, the poet

Ovid wrote: 'But still, the fates will leave me my voice, and by my voice I shall be known.' Do you want to be known? Do you have something to say? You have to have something to say if you expect people to be interested in your work. That means your life has to yield something to write about. Henry David Thoreau said, 'The mass of men lead lives of quiet desperation. What is called resignation is confirmed desperation. From the desperate city you go into the desperate country, and have to console yourself with the bravery of minks and muskrats.' What do you think he means? I don't live a life like that, do you? I sure as hell don't want to."

All day Claire thought about what Tyler had said, wondering if she was living in quiet desperation. It wasn't exactly quiet at the trailer, but sometimes she felt desperate. She also thought about Cherry, and said a prayer for her more than once. Cherry was beyond desperate. She was lost.

Tyler had given them an assignment. They had to write about a time when they had touched the face of God, whatever that meant to them. Claire found one of Toby's Blue Horse writing tablets and began to put her thoughts down with a violet Crayola.

Jackie Mackie

That Sunday, Jackie Mackie was volunteering in the toddler room at the Tabernacle. Sam had not fully recovered from the attack on his nervous system and Claire did not like the idea of Jackie Mackie being in the same room with him. Jackie had worn another outfit that made her breasts seem like her most important character asset. She put Claire's small breasts to shame, and, the thing was, Claire had not felt any significant breast inferiority since high school, but now she had every reason to believe that Jackie Mackie was on the prowl for her husband. Did she even care? Was the rumbling of jealousy she felt a result of her love for Karl or just knee-jerk jealousy? She'd seen female dogs straddling each other just to get the last pee before their bladders emptied. Is that what this was? A peeing contest?

"Oh hi, Claire," Jackie said when she saw them at the door. "Hi Sam." Jackie wore a big smile, her voice bright. How did she know Sam's name? She had never kept him in the toddler room before, had she? "How're ya'll doin'?" She directed the question to Claire.

"We're all good," Claire said tersely.

"You know, you n' me should get coffee sometime, Claire. I'd love to get to know ya better." Jackie put her warm hand on Claire's arm.

"Yeah, well give me a call sometime and we'll do that,"

Claire said. "You know about Sam, right? About his condition?"

"No, not really, I mean, I heard something happened and he had to go to Duke."

"He has myasthenia gravis. It attacks his nervous system. He's on meds so he's a little sluggish. He just needs to take it easy."

"Okay, that's no problem. We can read some books, how would you like that, Sam?" Sam just looked at her. It was not his habit to speak to adults.

All through the service, Claire thought about Jackie Mackie and what was going on in the toddler room. She knew that Jackie was not going to do anything to Sam. It wasn't even about Sam. It was about sharing someone she loved with someone she hated. Sam was a sweetie, very tender-hearted, and Jackie, who didn't have any children, was getting to enjoy her sweet boy. That gnawed at her.

Monday morning Claire dropped by the Scotsman. Tommy's truck with its ladder rack and buckets of plaster and paint in the bed was parked at one of the pumps, a black hose feeding it gas. He was inside getting a Monster energy drink from the upright case.

"Hey girl," he called to get her attention.

"Hi Tommy. What's up with you?"

"I've got some good news. Marla and I broke up. Now all you gotta do is break up with Karl, and we can get together. Or we can get together anyway."

"It's too early for your shit, Tommy. I need a Coke."

"You don't seem surprised about Marla."

"Were you surprised?"

"Not really. She's too smart for me."

"Oh, and I'm not? I'm just dumb enough for Tommy Hendrix?"

"How's Sam doin'?" Tommy asked in an effort to change the subject.

"He's doin' okay. You seen Johnny C lately?"

"Yeah, you need the hook up? Get your Coke and meet me at the truck."

Claire hadn't talked to Marla in two days but she expected a visit. Sure enough, Marla popped in after work to tell her that she had broken up with Tommy. Karl wasn't home yet. They shared a joint on the back porch while the boys watched the Cartoon Channel.

"You glad you did it?" Claire asked.

"It was about time. He was getting obnoxious."

"I can see that, yeah, I can easily see that with him. He's always been obnoxious."

"I don't think I'll ever find anyone that's right for me."

"Like a true soulmate, you mean?"

"Yeah."

"What about Jeb?" Claire asked.

"I don't know. He so hard to read."

"I think soulmates are hard to come by," Claire said. "And all men got them wanderin' eyes. Karl's got eyes for that woman at church."

"That Jackie woman?"

"Yeah. *Jackie Mackie.*" The way Claire said it you'd have thought Jackie was a slug, or a snake, something that slunk around and lived under a rock.

"What are you going to do?" Marla asked.

"What can I do?" Claire sucked the last burn out of the tiny roach and flicked the speck of paper into the yard.

The courthouse was empty on Sunday except for a security guard in dark blue slacks and a light blue shirt dotted with tiny holes from cigar sparks, a black man who had the subservient attitude of a slave, a man broken and trained to hoe the white man's rows and be polite about it. He wouldn't look Claire, Karl or George in the eye. He just unlocked the big doors to hear their request.

"We're supposed to meet Judge Carrington today," George said. He had arranged the Sunday meeting as a reaction to the letter that had been delivered by registered mail to their home on Friday demanding that Toby and Sam be turned over to social services on Monday by order of the court.

"I guess that'd be alright," the guard said in a slow drawl. "The judge is in her chambers." He swung the door open for them, locked it behind them, and began to walk down the long corridor, its shiny, tile floors casting elongated shadows. Claire looked at George, who had a very somber expression, as if they were walking to the electric chair. Perhaps he hadn't done this before and didn't know what to expect, perhaps he was intimidated by this encounter with the judicial system, which, in Sampson County, was the domain of good ol' boys. Claire had never seen a black man look so pale. When the registered letter had arrived, George was the first person she called. If the court took her little soldiers away, she would freak out.

The guard knocked gently on the judge's door, then turned the knob. The judge, a middle-aged woman with dyed-blonde hair, sitting at her desk on the far side of the room, studying her computer screen, did not look up.

"Do you think it's safe to give out your credit card information over the Internet" The judge asked. "I just ordered a cocktail dress from Overstock dotcom. I have no idea why. It was on sale. I'll probably look like Buddha's wife in it. Of course, he didn't have a wife did he. Or do we even know? I haven't bought a new dress in over a year. I don't even need a cocktail dress. I don't even drink. Oh, maybe a glass of Pinot Noir now and then, but not cocktails. Who can say no to a good Pinot? That rhymed, didn't it, but not on purpose. I guess the point is ... well ... what do you think of it?" She motioned for Claire to walk around the desk. Claire did as beckoned. The dress was red with elegant lines. The judge was attractive, however, her body shape was not the shape required for the dress. She would look ridiculous in a dress like that.

"I think it's pretty. I'd wear it," Claire said.

"You're a young girl with a figure. I'm ... well, forget it. Enough of that. I paid for it so it's too late. What's the point, they've got my credit card number. Now, you asked for this meeting didn't you? What do you have to say that is so important I had to come down here on Sunday? You may go around to the other side of my desk now young

146

lady." Claire walked around the desk and stood beside Karl and George. "You may sit down," the judge said. George pulled an extra chair over so the three of them could sit facing the judge. It was then that the judge noticed the guard.

"Eugene, come over here and get some candy." On her desk sat the scales of justice, and the trays of the scales held small bowls filled with colorful hard candy in cellophane wrappers.

"No ma'am, I thank you though," Eugene said, backing toward the door. "I best go now and do my rounds."

"Eugene, please take some candy."

"Thank you ma'am but I best be on my way." He opened the door and slipped out.

"I have been working here for twenty years, and I've known Eugene for that long, and he never, ever takes candy." She looked at them. He is in that older generation of African-Americans who still remember black and white water fountains. We had them right here in this building.

"That's odd, isn't it, how he won't take any candy," Claire said.

"Yes, I think it is. Now, dear, tell me why you are here."

"Well, DSS wants to take my boys away, and it's because of a misunderstanding. They say that because we missed some parenting classes, we can't be their parents anymore."

"You'll always be their parents, dear," the judge said.

"Judge," George said, "the reason they missed the parenting classes is because one of their boys became ill and had to spend two weeks in the hospital in Durham."

"And frankly we forgot all about the classes because our

147

boy was so sick," Claire added.

"How is he now?" the judge asked.

"He's much better," Karl said.

"Is he in preschool?"

"Yes ma'am," Claire said. "He just has to take it real easy."

"What's the nature of his illness?"

"It's called myasthenia gravis," Claire said.

"That can be very serious. How old is your son?"

"He's five," Claire said.

"That must have been difficult for you, to see him fall ill with that."

"Yes ma'am."

"You love your children?"

"Yes ma'am."

"But something happened to get you in trouble with DSS."

"Yes ma'am. Mostly drinkin' and carryin' on."

"Carryin' on? What do you mean?"

"Fighting, me and Karl. Getting drunk and fighting," Claire said. "And I hit Toby with a baseball bat but only one time. With a plastic bat. On his leg."

"I feel like you're being honest with me."

"I'm tryin' to be." Claire looked her in the eye.

"George, what do you have to say about these two?"

"I've been observing the family for two months, so my observation isn't complete, but they seem to have created stability in the home. I haven't seen any signs of drug or alcohol use or parental abuse of the children."

"Well, I don't see why DSS needs to take your children

away and subject them to needless trauma. But I do have a few questions for you." Claire and Karl slipped forward an inch in their upholstered chairs. "Do you love each other?" They looked at each other.

"Yes ma'am," Claire said. Karl was surprised to hear her say it.

"And what about you, young man?"

"Yes," Karl answered. "I love her."

"Will you promise me to keep your family together and to keep it strong, so your children can experience a healthy emotional environment?" Claire and Karl shook their heads. "No drugs, no alcohol, no fighting?"

"No ma'am," Claire said. "I mean, we'll be good. Karl works at Walmart now and found Jesus and stopped drinking."

"What about you?"

"Me?

"Have you found Jesus?"

"Yes ma'am."

She looked at them skeptically. "Everybody finds Jesus when they get in enough trouble. Then they lose him again when the pull of drugs or alcohol sneaks back. It has a way of sneaking back, you know. If George reports anything like drugs or alcohol to DSS, and if I get wind of anything like that, I'll snatch those children out of the home in an instant. Do you understand?" They shook their heads again. "Okay, well that's that. George, I'm rescinding this order to appear tomorrow."

"Thank you, Judge." George said.

"Keep an eye on them," the judge said.

On their way out, Eugene saw them on his closed-circuit video system. He sat in a chair in a small room with a console of eight tiny black and white monitors and half a pot of coffee cooking on a Mister Coffee. He watched them walk silently down the corridor. They had no idea he was watching, just the way he watched over the entire courthouse every weekend when it was only an overworked judge or D.A., and the floor-polishers, who came in to disrupt his solitude.

Karl had been gone most of the day. He'd been looking for his father in Harrells or thereabouts. Claire was chopping slaw when he walked in holding five beers, the empty plastic six-pack loop hanging from a finger. He didn't say anything at first, just sat on the sofa and put the beer on the sofa beside him.

"Dad's gone."

"Gone? Gone where?" Claire asked. Karl sank backward on the worn-out sofa. "Karl?"

"Gone as in dead. They found him out in the woods leaning against a pear tree with a bunch of rotted pears all over the place and about a thousand bees. The coroner got stung three times trying to haul him out." His head drooped and he sighed. Claire sat beside him. "They couldn't find any foul play." Karl was clutching something so tight in his fist his knuckles were white.

"I'm sorry, honey," Claire said, stroking his arm. He opened his fingers. He was holding a Remington belt buckle.

150

"This the only thing they had left. They sold his whole apartment full of stuff to pay for the funeral."

"Who did?"

"A couple of his friends at the mill. They cremated him. They sold my grandpa's railroad watch and his double barrel, they sold Daddy's shoes, clothes, bowling ball, everything. They were still two hundred dollars short. I told 'em I'd send a check."

"I wish he'd left you something besides a buckle," Claire said, and popped open a beer. "Where is he now, his ashes, I mean?"

"They spread him on a little patch of grass in front of the bowling alley."

"The bowling alley?"

"A place called Memory Lanes. In Harrells."

"Never heard of it."

"Me either."

"I guess your daddy liked to bowl, huh?"

"That's what his buddies said. I didn't know that about him. Of course, I didn't really know him anyway."

Karl had never known a girl like Claire and never would again. She had given him the beauty of her youth, from the age of eighteen to twenty-six, and during that stretch he had become an alcoholic. He had abused her physically and mentally and given her nothing to live for except two babies. Two babies and a few bruises about every weekend. That was not fair to a girl as pretty as Claire. A girl who could've had somebody a lot better.

Ever since his father was found half-rotted leaning against the pear tree with enough bees buzzing around him to populate a farmer's hive, Karl hadn't been the same, not at all. He seemed to be daydreaming most of the time, adrift in his thoughts, and uncomfortable with sobriety. His job had lost its sheen. Everything had lost its sheen. With his father gone, he felt like he was all on his own, cut loose from his genetic moorings, and more unsure of himself than usual.

Ever since Jackie Mackie had met Karl, she'd fantasized about making love to him. He was not really her *type* but she thought he was sexy and he was definitely her *speed*.

She decided it was time for new tires. Sensing that she had a good opening, she wore a low-cut silk blouse and push-up leopard bra. The last time she'd gone after a married man, her timing was off. She played her trump card, sex, then he folded and ran back to his wife. But Karl was different. He was a good listener, and he connected with her. Claire wasn't where he was spiritually. What Karl really needed was a woman who shared his love of God and the church. God would forgive their rough beginning. Surely, God wanted Karl to be happy, and surely he frowned upon Claire's lifestyle. As an assistant manager at the 24-Hour Diner, Jackie offered financial stability to go with her emotional maturity and sensuality, a total package for Karl, if she could just get him to see it. He had told her that Claire was on to them. Yet all they had done was flirt. Jackie made her way to Tire n' Lube, where Karl waited behind the counter.

"Hey," she said, and she saw his eyes light up.

"Hi Jackie. What are you doing here?"

"I came for a set of Coopers. You do tires don't you?"

"Sure. We got good prices on our Coopers, too. Where's your car at, let's take a look see." They walked outside and Karl examined her tires. "R17s. You want whitewalls? You really don't need back tires. If you want you can wait a few months, you still got some tread on 'em."

"No, go ahead and give me four. I like to keep them all the same. I think the car drives better."

"No problem."

"Are you going to put them on?"

"I can do it if you want me to. We got Cesar, he's real fast. If you want, I can take my break while he does the work." Karl wrote up the order. Jackie could see she had him hooked, he wasn't even fighting the barb, probably didn't even feel it in his lip. They sat in the junk food alcove. Jackie was dismayed to see that he drank his coffee black. That was a bad sign.

"I've been thinking about you a lot, too much, really," Jackie said.

"Oh yeah, what have you been thinking?"

"How cute you are. I know I shouldn't tell you that. I know you're married, and we were just baptized and I know you and I both want to do the right thing. But what if God put us together at the Tabernacle for a reason?"

"I can see that."

"You can?"

"Yeah."

"What about your wife?" Jackie asked.

"She's going to school. I hardly ever see her."

"Are you still in love with her?"

"I'd have to say so."

"Do you find me attractive?" Jackie asked. She studied his face for anything that could help her understand him. "Because you make me hot you're so cute," she said with breathy emphasis.

"I do?" Karl was bewitched. He let his eyes fall to her breasts, realizing that it pleased her.

"What if ... what if we got a motel room, just for one night?"

"Sounds good to me if you think we should."

"I think we should. I'm up for anything, honey bear." There. She'd done it. She'd played her trump card.

The boys were still awake when Tommy dropped by the trailer. Claire opened the door carefully.

"What do you want?" she asked.

"I came to pay you a visit," Tommy said. "Something wrong with that?" He was dressed in black like Johnny Cash without a guitar over his shoulder.

"Why are you here? What if Karl was home?"

"I'm just killin' time's all. What, can't you let me in?"

"My boys ain't down yet. You drive around awhile and I'll put 'em down. Come back in half an hour." Tommy stepped off the stoop. "And hey, pick up some beer why don'tcha."

She put the boys down and made them say their prayers. Tommy came back in a half hour like he'd been told.

"Where's Karl?" Tommy asked, settling onto the sofa.

"He's camping out with a buddy from work," Claire said. "They're going fishing and shit like that." She handed him a Corona after putting the rest of the six-pack in the fridge. She screwed hers open.

"Oh, must be fun, going fishin' like that with a buddy from work," Tommy said.

"You fish?"

"Sure, sometimes from the pier at Long Beach. I did that when I was a kid. I even caught a shark out there one night, about three feet long. I just remembered something, when I was real little I wanted to be a oceanographer or marine biologist."

"You could still do it," Claire said. "You can get a student loan."

"But I don't have the grades. Never took that test you gotta take either, and if I did I'd flunk it, that's how I wound up at the mill, you know. Summers I worked there so I had a good job when I got out of high school, and my grades sucked, so that's why I'm here talking to you tonight. Otherwise, I might be out on a ship, or underwater looking at a fish or an octopus or something of that nature."

"You got any weed?" Claire asked.

"Of course."

"Let's go outside," she said. They shared a joint on the back patio. When the sun set in Sampson County, it was so dark you could see the craters on the moon. There was no light pollution from city buildings or streetlamps.

"You come over here to try to get in my britches, Tommy?"

"Hell no."

"What for then?"

"Well, I wouldn't mind gettin' in them britches, to be honest, but what I really come to tell you, well, you ain't gonna like it."

"Why, what is it? Damnitall, Tommy, you better tell me."

"I saw Karl's truck at the motel out 29 near Clinton."

"You what?"

"Uh-huh."

"The motel?"

"Uh-huh."

"You sure it was his?"

"Uh-huh. Well, that's not all, Claire. I pulled in to where Karl was parked. I figured he probably took a room. I looked in the window and saw him in there with a woman."

"You're lyin'. You're a lyin' sonofabitch." Her face was hot, she was feeling flustered by anger.

"No. I'm sorry, but it's the truth."

"What possessed you to do that?"

"Aside from the fact that I think Karl is an asshole?"

"Who was the woman? I'll bet it was Jackie Mackie from the Tabernacle. Sure it was. Of course it was. Damn him. Damn him. Damn him to fuckin' hell!"

Claire packed the boys in the Wrangler. With Tommy's headlights in her rearview, she drove them to her mother and father's.

"I'll explain it later!" She yelled on her way back to Tommy's pickup. They drove to the motel and parked two doors down from Karl's Chevy S10.

She stared at the curtains in the window, straining to see a glimpse of Jackie Mackie, or even her shadow.

"I should go in there and beat the shit out of him the way he used to do me."

"You don't have to whisper, Claire. Nobody's gonna hear you."

"What do you think I should do?"

"I don't know. I've got a gun under the seat if you want to kill 'em."

"Do you really?"

"Yep."

"Lemme see it."

"I'm not gonna show it to you, you might flip out and really do it."

"This is not fair. He's in there screwin' his brains out and I'm just sitting here doin' nothin'."

"Why did we come here, because you didn't believe me?" Tommy eased his arm around her shoulders.

"I had to see it to believe it, to experience the reality of it." She pushed his arm away. "Stop that."

"Well, now you know the reality of it."

"Yeah, now I know," Claire said.

Tommy slept with her that night, but he didn't take his clothes off. He woke up looking like a rumpled Johnny Cash, but she let him share her bed because she decided she needed his arm around her after all. In high school, he'd asked her to the harvest dance but she thought he was obnoxious and not that cool. He'd always been the kind of friend who shows up at every party, at The Inferno, whenever you have a need for weed, but you kind of take them for granted because they are about as shiftless, jobless and aimless as you are.

Jackie came to see her that afternoon.

"What do you want?" Claire asked at the door.

"I want just a minute of your time, darlin'," Jackie said. She was dressed up like she was going to a cookout or to church.

"Watch out for the toys," Claire said, opening the door. She didn't give a rat's ass that the trailer looked like a dump. Jackie scanned the interior of her home with judgmental eyes. Claire could smell her spearmint gum.

"Let me tell you why I'm here," Jackie said. "I heard there was a rumor being spread around church about me and Karl. I want you to know those ugly rumors are flat out lies. I'm not interested in your husband."

"You're not, huh? Well that's good."

"He's a nice man and all, but I'm not interested in him."

"I was at the motel last night," Claire said.

"You were *what?*"

"I was at the motel. I know what you're doing. I don't know why you came here to lie to me right in my face, but I know you're screwin' my husband you fuckin' bitch, and know what? You can have him." Claire picked up a plastic baseball bat. She had used it many times to pop the boys, now she was going to pop Jackie. She swung the bat through the air. It had a built-in whistle. The tip of the bat swished by Jackie's nose so close it blew her hair back. She made for the door. Claire brought the bat across her rump and it made a loud smack. Jackie reared back as if to swing a fist at Claire but Claire was too quick. She hit Jackie across the side of the head with the bat. Jackie grabbed the flimsy door of the trailer and rushed out. Claire stepped onto the stoop and watched Jackie run. She ran like a girl, not like an athlete, not like Claire ran. Claire could have run her down and smacked her again, the thought passed through her mind, thoughts of tackling and pummeling, eye-gouging, but soon enough Jackie's new Coopers were spraying gravel as she spun down the driveway.

Claire knew the divorce would hurt because no matter how disappointed she was in Karl, he was her husband and the father of the boys and their souls had been tethered together for seven miserable years. She was sorry he came from a long line of bums, wife-abusers, adulterers and criminals, but if it was her problem now, even after Jesus had been given a chance in his life, then it would always be her problem, unless she decided to change things, and she had.

Since they had to take Sam to Duke for his checkup, she went ahead and brought it up. They were in the sunroom of the Children's Wing when she broke the news.

"Do you love her?" Claire asked point blank.

"Who?"

"You know who. Jackie Mackie."

"I don't think I do."

"Then what is it? Just the sex?"

"I guess."

"And what about me? Where do I fit in now, for you I mean?"

"I don't know."

"Your pitifulness is getting old."

"Tough. Pitiful is all I'm good for today. Truth is, Claire, I'm struggling with some demons."

"Well, I'm going to have to leave you with your demons, because I don't want to fight them anymore, I just want out."

"Huh?"

"Out, I want out of our marriage. I think you should leave because I want the singlewide. You're the one who had to go running around on me with Jackie Mackie."

"Okay," he said, and finally glanced up at her. "I think Jackie might let me move in."

That night, Tommy swooped in again like some kind of prescient bird. He brought a cold six-pack and they sat on the patio drinking. The boys were staying over with J.J. and Big Eddie, so she was free. She made some Hamburger Helper. They smoked some weed. She remembered what Marla had said about Tommy's lovemaking skills, and since he was down on his luck and she was having distracting sexual thoughts, she decided to make love to him. She knew it was a mistake before she even kissed him. While they were cuddled in bed, Howie was dumping Karl out in front of her parents' house. He was bleeding from his nose and mouth and just barely able to crawl to the door and bang on it. Luckily, he didn't wake the boys.

"Who did this to you?" J.J. asked. Big Eddie had dragged him into the kitchen and propped him in a chair.

"Howie. He pulled me over. He was driving his

160

cruiser." Karl mumbled the words because his lips were puffy. "He used his blue light. He was in his deputy uniform for godsake."

"What'd he do it for?" Big Eddie asked.

"Hell if I know," Karl said. "He put on some of those linesman's gloves and went off on me. What could I do? He had a gun. Crazy sumbitch." J.J. handed him an iced tea. "I don't understand why God let this happen to me after I gave him my life."

"Maybe it's his judgement side making up for some past sins. Some past beatings," J.J. said.

"Why would a deputy have linesman's gloves?" Karl asked.

"Who knows," Big Eddie said, "maybe he carries them in case he finds a live power line or something. But honestly boy, I think God used Howie to take out his holy wrath on you." Big Eddie winked at J.J. while she dabbed the scarlet blood oozing from Karl's face.

The next morning, Pastor Owens knocked on the trailer door. He told Claire he was looking for Karl, he'd heard about the beating. The pastor was standing in the den when Tommy walked into the kitchen to get coffee. He poured his coffee and went onto the porch without saying a word to the pastor, as if he didn't exist. Claire walked to the sofa and sat down. The pastor sat beside her.

"Claire, something seems out of place here, and it pains me as I think about it. I mean, it pains and perplexes. That young man belongs somewhere else, and Karl belongs here in this home, not at Jackie's. So how might we go about getting everyone set straight again in their proper homes?" Tommy stood behind the sliding glass door smoking a Vantage. "Claire, you've tasted the love God offers. Don't stop now. Don't return to your own vomit like a dog. You know dogs do that."

"That's gross."

"But it's how people do. We like to wallow in our sin and ignorance. Claire, Karl says you've got a drinking problem." Claire stared at her knees. "If you are an alcoholic, we know that it leads to moral decay. It will eventually make you a person with what I call *soul rot*. Understand? That's how it always works. I've seen it a hundred times. Is that fella one of your drinking buddies?" She glanced up at Tommy. He looked like a dark apparition behind glass, glaring at the pastor.

"He got fired from the mill."

"A lot of people did. The whole town's smarting from that closing. Claire, what are you going to do?" Tommy slid the patio door open but didn't step into the room, just stood there at the intersection of August heat and cool, conditioned air.

"You coming in? You're running up my electrical," Claire said.

"Not yet. Not until he's gone. It's hot as a fucking furnace out here though."

"Tommy, he's a pastor."

"I know," Tommy said. "So?"

Pastor Owens left without getting a decision from her.

He knew he was losing her to the nefarious forces vying to control her, but now all he could do was pray and hope she didn't slide too far down sin's slippery slope.

Singer Mountain

Aisha, Claire, Livia and Ember parked at the base of Singer Mountain. The hike took over two hours. It was rocky and rooty, parts of the trail had deep, washed out ruts, at times it got so steep they had to use trailside trees to pull themselves up. Aisha climbed like a goat, but Ember and Livia were out of shape, huffing and puffing. Claire suggested they take a break every few minutes. She didn't want Ember popping a blood vessel. The veins in her neck were standing up like the roots they were tripping over. The djembe strapped to her knapsack only added to her burden. Livia kept wearing a smile, wiping away her sweat with a red bandana. She had her hair braided and pulled back into two pigtails.

They had brought Sangria and weed but all Claire wanted after climbing the mountain was an ice cold Corona or Cherry Vanilla Dr. Pepper.

It took Aisha and Ember no time at all to set up the tents and start a fire, even though it was only three o'clock in the afternoon and the sun was blistering. "A fire will keep bears away," Aisha explained.

"What are we going to do now?" Claire asked.

"We've got our drums, and our poems. Drums and poems," Aisha said. She started to chant, "Drums and poems, poems and drums," over and over until Claire wanted to push her off a cliff.

Livia and Claire walked along a ridge that looked out over a deep ravine with a whitewater stream running through it. They had both sweated through their clothes and the breeze on the ridge felt good.

"Isn't it beautiful," Livia said.

"Yeah, it is," Claire said.

"I'd like to live in the wilderness, I think, except for the bears and snakes. I don't mind bugs. I don't like them but I don't mind them."

"I'm the same way," Claire said. She was glad she'd found something she had in common with Livia, because she was probably the wealthiest girl Claire had ever met. Her father owned a Hardees franchise and they had a cottage at Holden Beach.

"Guess what we found?" Ember had walked up behind them. "A spring. Come on." They thrashed though the underbrush to an opening in the forest where a dark pool thirty feet wide reflected the canopy of green over their heads. Aisha was sitting on a rock unstrapping her hiking boots.

"What are you going to do?" Claire asked.

"I'm going in. It's cold as hell, but I don't care," Aisha said. Claire dipped her hand in the clear water. It was cold as a glass of ice water. Aisha started taking off her boots.

"Why not," Claire said.

They stepped carefully into the pool, its bottom covered in slimy leaves, but the water felt so refreshing. Aisha dipped down and let it cover her lower half, then pulled off her T-shirt and sank to her shoulders.

"Are we going skinny-dipping?" Livia asked.

"It feels great," Aisha said, swirling her hands just under the surface. Livia kicked off her shorts and peeled off her T-shirt and went in in her underpants. Claire followed her example.

"I'm so fat," Ember said. "Ya'll have to promise not to laugh."

"We won't laugh. Do it," Claire said. Ember kept her shorts on but stripped off her T-shirt and unhooked the bra that held her enormous breasts. She made the funniest face as she lowered her body down into the emerald pool.

They swam and sunbathed until they all agreed it was time to make dinner. They built up the fire and let it burn down until they had a pile of coals they could cook their tin foil dinners on. Aisha had made up the tin foil packets with turkey burgers, potatoes, carrots and onions, a little olive oil and rosemary. Claire wished she could be like Aisha: smart, capable, artistic, articulate. She liked the way Aisha encouraged her and the others to write. She wasn't all about herself. She seemed to feed her own life with the love she could create among friends.

When night fell, they built a fire so big it almost ignited the tree branches above them. They read their poems and played the djembe, drank two bottles of wine, shared a joint and ate enough smores to make themselves sick. It was like some kind of religious bonding experience, and the mystical power of poetry provided the extra ribbons of glue.

Aisha and Claire were sharing a two-person dome tent, snuggled into their sleeping bags, facing each other, when Aisha said something strange.

"Claire," Aisha said, "sometimes I feel like I'm not really here, like I'm just a dream of myself."

"That's weird, isn't it," Claire said. "How could that be?"

"Yeah. It's weird, but I don't mean I'm really dreaming all of this, just that life feels dream-like and insubstantial sometimes."

"What does that mean, 'insubstantial?'" Claire asked.

"Ephemeral, like we're ghosts. You know, all we're made of is energy, that's all, just energy, that's what the whole universe is made of, energy in different forms."

"Okay," Claire said. She didn't know where Aisha was going with the conversation. Then Aisha reached out and touched Claire's cheek, letting her fingers rest there. "You are made of protons and electrons whirling around each other, and so am I. Isn't that amazing. But you are different than me, Claire, you live your life differently. You actually *live* it."

"What do you do?" Claire asked. She was beginning to wonder if Aisha was a lesbian, because she was stroking her cheek so gently and lovingly, the way Claire touched her boys' cheeks while they were sleeping.

"I don't live my life, I simply endure it," Aisha said. "And you know why? I can't get outside myself." Now Claire could see that Aisha was just drunk and melancholy. She took her hand and removed it from her face but they continued to hold hands as Aisha talked. "Things happened to me when I was a little girl, and my little self was forced to retreat, to hide, and when the little me stepped back from reality, she could only go inside her mind, so that's what

167

she did, she went inside her mind to search for herself in there away from anyone who could hurt her."

"Who hurt you?" Claire asked.

"My mother and father mainly. There was a lot of discord in our family and I seemed to be the cause of it. I was a little hellion, and they tried to tame me, but they couldn't. That's why I had to leave home."

"Aren't you glad you got away? You've been able to live your own life, not like me, I started making babies and look at me now, I'm broken up from my husband, he's having an affair, I'm having an affair, everything is upside down now, and my boys are not going to have a whole family."

"I lot of people get divorced," Aisha said. "Marriage is frickin' hard as hell."

"Do you want to get married one day?" Claire asked.

"Sure, one day, when I find the right man. When and if."

"I think you're drunk and that's why you're thinking all these deep thoughts," Claire said. "You're a good person, and you're smart, and you can write really good."

"You're like a little porcelain doll," Aisha said. She put her hand on Claire's face again. "You're so beautiful."

"I don't like being called a doll," Claire said, remembering back to her Barbie days. She was beyond being a "doll." Just the word itself was so childish.

Aisha smiled, "I like your face. Your skin is so smooth. If I were gay I might fall for you." Aisha olled over and looked up at the ceiling of the tent. She could see stars through the sheer vent in the dome. "Everything in the universe is made of energy, but we can think and feel. We might be the only thing in the whole universe that has consciousness, that is aware of itself. Isn't that amazing. It's hard not to believe in God sometimes. I know you believe, and something in me wants to believe, but another part of me doesn't see how it's possible."

"Our pastor says it's something you know in your heart," Claire said. "Because God is love, so, if you feel his love, you know it's him."

"That's a nice idea. Do you pray?" Aisha asked. "Do you talk to God?"

"Sure. Except lately I've been feeling guilty about Tommy, you know, sleeping with him when I'm still married. Even though Karl's screwing around and being a complete asshole, I don't think that's a good excuse for me to be doing what I'm doing, so I've been kind of avoiding God."

"Do you think he's going to strike you dead for what you're doing?" Aisha asked.

"No," Claire said. "I don't think so. If I did, I wouldn't be doing it, would I?"

"I've never been to a party with a teacher before," Claire said upon entering Tyler's house. He had invited his poetry and short story classes over for a cookout. Most of the students were outside where the grill was smoking. The interior of the house was furnished with primitive antiques and there were a lot of weird pictures, weird to Claire anyway.

"These pieces were done by people with handicaps,"

Tyler explained. "It's an obsession of mine. People with handicaps fascinate me. It can be mental or physical. This one was done by a woman in the throes of deep depression, this was painted by a boy with spina bifida. He painted it with his mouth. Well, I mean he held the brush between his teeth."

"What about that one?" Claire pointed at a painting that was done in splashes of primary colors.

"Actually, that was painted by a lowland gorilla." Tyler laughed. "I paid a hundred and twenty dollars for it."

"You got ripped off," Claire said.

"Yeah, maybe I did."

"What about that one?" She pointed at a watercolor of a lake.

"That's White Lake in Elizabethtown. It was formed by meteorite impact. Crater lakes are another obsession of mine. That was painted by my girlfriend, my *former* girlfriend."

"Was she handicapped?"

"No, she was fine, I mean, she was healthy, normal."

"Why is she your former girl?"

"I don't know, people change. She wanted to go to medical school, I wanted to write."

"Why do you like to write?"

"Why do I write, or like to write, hmm, that's a good question. Why do I breathe? I love words, Claire, and I love what's possible with words, the malleability of language, you know, that kind of thing."

"Okay," Claire said. "I never heard that word before, but that sounds like a good answer to me, and anyway I'm so new at it. Do you have a girlfriend now?"

"Claire, you are very direct aren't you."

"Is that good, being direct?"

"It's not a bad thing. Yes, I do have a girlfriend. Her name is Elaine. She's coming over later."

Claire and Tyler walked outside. The students, a few of whom were older than Tyler, were drinking beer and talking. There were some guys from the short story class and Hector from their poetry class. Livia, Aisha and Ember were there. Claire was glad she'd dressed up. Some of the boys were cute. A boy named Ryan Dorsey, a few years younger than she was, maybe 20, introduced himself and offered to get her a beer. He was one of those people who just looks smart, like Tyler. He could probably be a teacher or doctor, a lawyer, some kind of professional. Looked like he came from a good home with smart parents. Somebody passed a joint around and Tyler didn't seem to mind. Claire had already learned that he was liberal. He didn't like Bush or the war in Iraq.

"Do you want to go inside?" Ryan asked. They went in and sat down on the sofa. "I've heard you're a good poet," Ryan said. "I hope you'll read something tonight."

"I was thinking I might," Claire said. "If I can get up the nerve. What kinds of stuff do you write about?"

"I write about whatever interests me. Everything interests me, so I write about whatever comes up, whatever finds its way out of my subconscious. What about you? What do you write about?"

"Dreams usually. Not just night dreams but day dreams, too. Just stuff I see and think about." She could see that he

171

liked her. His eyes were flirting with her.

"What are you doing in Newton Grove?" Claire asked. "You didn't go to Sampson High did you?"

"No. My mother lives here. She's sick, so I came down to stay with her. I had been going to UNC-Greensboro."

"What's wrong with your mom?" Claire asked.

"Cancer. But she's adamantly opposed to death, so I have no idea how long I'll be here." Aisha came over and plopped down between Claire and Ryan. She was high, loopy.

"Look at you two," she said, grinning.

"And look at you," Claire said.

"I think I need food, I've already had two beers," Aisha said. Ryan looked at Claire as if to say, "What the hell is her problem?"

"I'm intruding aren't I? Sorry." Aisha sprang up nimbly and headed toward the kitchen.

"I think some of the people here are questionable in terms of their sanity tonight," Ryan said.

"I know she is," Claire said. Her hand brushed against Ryan's. He stroked her arm with the tips of his fingers. His touch made her shiver.

"Are you cold?" he asked.

"No, you did that."

"Sorry."

"No, it's okay," Claire said, "it's just ... I'm older than you."

"Does that matter?"

"I guess not. Maybe we should get a hamburger." Claire stood up. It took a few seconds to get steady on her feet.

After dinner, they sat around Tyler's den and read their poems and short stories. Everyone had five minutes to read if they wanted to. Ryan read a story about his brother who had a speech impediment when he was little. Ryan was the only person who could understand him, and they had their own private world.

Claire read a poem about a frozen waterfall she had dreamed about. In the dream she was climbing a snow-covered hill and came to a waterfall that had turned to ice. She climbed onto the ice-encased rocks. She looked closely at the waterfall and saw water flowing through a sheath of ice, she broke off a piece and freed the water to find a new way down, drops splattering into the air and turning into snowflakes. The snowflakes covered her until she disappeared from sight.

"I think your dream has psychological implications," Ryan said later. They were in Tyler's backyard and Ryan was smoking a clove cigarette.

"What does that mean?"

"It means it reveals what's inside you."

"I don't think so. It's just a dream."

"I think there's more to it."

"Like what?" Claire asked, as Ryan blew out a stream of spicy smoke.

"It's about transformation, you are an agent of transformation in the poem."

"You're nuts. Why can't it just be a dream?"

"Maybe because it's more than a dream. Dreams often have spiritual or psychological significance."

"You probably read a book about it."

"I did actually."

"You're too smart for community college. What are you going to do when you get out?"

"I'd like to go back to UNC-Greensboro for an MFA."

"Is that for writers?"

"It's the master of fine arts program."

"I thought writing was a liberal art?"

"It is. It's both liberal and fine. Of course, you don't have to go to school to learn how to write. I had a professor at UNC-G who believed that all it took to become a writer was five hundred pages."

"That's a lot. For me that would be five hundred poems."

"Claire, why don't we go to my place after the party."

"Your place?"

"I want to make love to you."

"You what? Wow. I can't believe what you just said, I can't believe my ears."

"I know. I don't believe in wasting time." He blew out another blue stream of clove smoke and looked at her as she scrutinized his offer.

"I'll go home with you," she said, her smile revealing only a glimmer of how good his offer made her feel.

Tyler's girlfriend, Elaine, was not what Claire expected. She was not intelligent-looking. Truth was, Tyler had given up on intelligent women who knew what they wanted out of life and would crush his ambitions to get it. He had opted for a country girl with good teeth and nice tits. Elaine worked at the Southern Market, Claire had seen her there a hundred times. She did the ringing up.

"I know you," Elaine said when Tyler introduced them. "You got them two handsome boys."

"That's right. How are you doing?" Claire asked.

"Pretty well I guess except my arches hurt like hell. That's wild you're in Tyler's class. Are you a writer?"

"Yep."

"Imagine that, who woulda guessed."

Ryan's house was an enormous brick mansion. Turns out his father Raymond Dorsey had owned the local hosiery mill and sold it to Burlington Industries back when textiles were still profitable. Raymond was dead but his wife had stayed in the house, living the life of a wealthy widow in a small town, playing bridge, growing roses, holding Christmas parties, and summering at their other house in Wilmington before her cancer diagnosis.

Claire looked around the living room while Ryan checked on his mother. She could hear them down the hallway, and the TV playing in the old woman's room. It was past twelve o'clock. Maybe his mother was one of those women who never turns the TV off. The furniture was antique, expensive-looking, unfriendly. Claire sat on the edge of a chair. The air in the room seemed to be more transparent than usual. She realized she didn't want to be there. Her high had worn off and she felt normal, even melancholic. Ryan was taking forever.

She found the kitchen and turned on the light. An antique butcher block from a Brooklyn deli occupied the center of the room. Claire looked in the fridge and found a Heinekin. She twisted the top off and took a long swallow.

The only food she could find was a jar of olives.

"Hungry?" Ryan asked. "I'll fix some breakfast if you want." He walked up to her, brushed back her hair, kissed her cheek. "You want me to?"

He fixed omelets and toast. She'd never tasted an omelet that good, even at Dennys. They talked more about writing. When they finally got around to making love, they did it in his parents' bedroom, since his mother was in a small room downstairs. The master bedroom had a huge bed with a down comforter. After Ryan caught his breath, they screwed again. Claire wasn't used to doing it twice in a row. Karl would just roll over and pass out. Ryan was a good lover, even better than Tommy. He really wanted to please her, but when he did, and she let out a small scream, he clamped his hand over her mouth. Then he held her, the way lovers do in the movies, with her head on his shoulder, stroking her hair. He told her how pretty she was and his tender words made her feel complete.

Ryan did not want his mother to know Claire was in the house. He explained that it would make her ask questions and upset her needlessly. So Claire left quietly in the morning and drove to her parents' house.

Big Eddie was in the carport putting new spark plugs in the riding mower, the boys were on the floor of the den watching TV and J.J. was just getting off the phone to the nursing home when Claire entered the kitchen.

"Mother's not doing well, I'm going to have to go over there and straighten things out," J.J. said. "I see you had a big night. Karl called looking for you. I told him you were sleeping here because you came in late from your poetry party, then he called this morning and I told him you weren't up yet. I hope you appreciate all my lying."

"I do, Momma, believe me I do."

"Okay, well, I suppose that baptism didn't take. I'm sorry, that was mean. But I do think you need to set the right example for your boys. Your separation is hard enough for them, now, with all your gallivanting, I'm sure they feel like a tornado's hit. You don't want them to think their mother is a loose woman."

"I am a loose woman, Momma."

"Just try to hide it from them, Claire. Toby said Tommy Hendricks had been over to the trailer. Is that so? *Is that so, Claire?*" Claire quickly collected the boys' things as J.J. followed behind her. "You aren't going to answer me are you, so it must be true. Are you sleeping with him? Is that your way of getting back at Karl? Do you even want to salvage your marriage? Karl's a decent man, now that he's at Walmart, and that Hendricks boy is a drug dealer."

" Momma, the woman Karl is screwin', Jackie Mackie, is a woman from church. How decent is that? And Tommy just sells a little weed now and then."

"Oh good God, Claire."

"Good God, what, Momma? I've finally got a life and I'm not looking back, I'm not going back to the way I was. I'll never go back to that, to being a stupid redneck." Her mother grabbed her by the wrist, her eyes pinched tight in anger.

"You can't escape who you are, Claire. You can't run away from your roots. Roots is roots."

"I can escape if I want to, Momma. There's more to

life than Newton Grove, a lot more." She jerked away and ran to the Wrangler. The seat was so hot you could fry an egg on it. She sat there, fighting back the convulsions that were trying to overtake her. Damitall, why did she always let her mother get to her that way?

The Wolf Pup

Having survived chemo, Helen Dorsey now used her illness as an opportunity to buy wigs. She had nine or ten different styles and colors on styrofoam heads sitting on the surfaces of her bedroom, like visitors waiting to speak their turn, yet with nothing to say, except "Wear me, wear me." She would take her time walking among them, but once she made up her mind, she plucked the wig from its perch, slipped it on and wore it until bedtime. The next day, she would choose another one, and, though no one noticed, because no one was there, each wig altered her personality perceptively. If her husband had been there, he would have noticed it, but he had died of a massive coronary in 1995. Ryan didn't notice, he had been ignoring her since high school, and most of her friends were dead. But she lived in a different world, a world of make believe, and enjoyed pretending she was Hedy Lamarr or Lana Turner or Barbara Stanwick.

She was cared for by a tag team of home health nurses that Ryan made sure were well compensated. His mother was no fun, especially when it came to the hired help. Knowing she was looked after, Ryan could forget about her ninety-nine percent of the time.

"These local girls are nothing but trouble, nothing but a waste of time," Helen told him. "Nothing but hicks." Spying from her groundfloor window, she had seen Claire leave that first morning, "Don't do this to me, Ryan, please," Helen had pleaded, "I don't have the time or the patience for it. And don't you dare get her pregnant, don't you *dare*. She will bleed us for every dime we have. These hicks are dangerous people, darling."

Claire had made Ryan her secret boyfriend. He needed to keep her secret from Helen, and Claire needed to keep him secret from Karl, even though Karl had left her. Besides, she didn't want J.J. to know she was sleeping around even though that was becoming her reputation, a mostly undeserved reputation, she felt, since Aisha claimed she had slept with sixteen guys and even had a list, and Ryan was only the fourth man she'd had sex with. Steve Autry in eleventh grade, Karl, Tommy, and Ryan, that was it.

She was in the big master bed with Ryan one evening at six o'clock, before the summer sun had even thought about setting, when they heard Helen yelling for help. They rushed downstairs. Claire stayed back, just outside Helen's bedroom door, while Ryan went in. Helen was in the bathroom. She had fallen in the shower. She seemed frightened, like a cornered racoon, but it may have been her dementia. She didn't seem to recognize Ryan but she knew he was a man and she was terribly embarrassed for him to see her naked. So Ryan asked Claire to come in. Helen was not wearing a wig and looked like some kind of alien life form.

"Are you hurt?" Claire asked. "Does anything hurt?"

"No, no, I'm fine. I'm fine, just get me up," Helen insisted. "You're that girl, aren't you?"

180

"I'm that girl," Claire admitted. She knew how old people break their hips and wanted to be sure Helen could stand up on her own.

"If her hip was broken, I think she'd be in terrible pain," Ryan said.

"Okay, let's get you up," Claire said. She had to bend over and grip Helen around the waist. "Try to get your feet under you, work with me here," Claire said. She was able to get Helen to her feet, though she was wobbly and clutched Claire's arm and the shower door handle to right herself. As she stepped from the shower onto the tile floor of the bathroom, Helen put so much weight on the door handle that the door popped from its hinges. The door tettered and shattered against the toilet as Helen's feet slipped out from under her. Claire tried to catch her but Helen hit the floor, landing on her butt. She curled up, crying pitifully, her flesh, white as cream, decorated with tiny shards of glass plastered all over her thighs, her hands quivering like dying fish, and screamed, "Get that redneck bitch out of my sight, get her out of my sight, Charles, she's trying to kill me!!!"

Claire left the bathroom and went to the kitchen. She was not going to be talked to like that by anyone. She found a bottle of Jewel of Russia in the freezer, poured some in a glass and took a gulp. A half hour passed before Ryan came looking for her.

"I think she's going to be okay. I called one of her nurses. She's only got some tiny cuts from the glass, thank God."

"I don't really care. I'm going home," Claire said.

Jackie and Karl lay in bed letting the air conditioner dry the sweat of lovemaking. She touched the small scar on his back. It was shaped like an arrowhead or greater than symbol.

"What's that?" Jackie asked. "How'd you get it? Looks like a scar."

"You know what, I was married to Claire for six years and she never wanted me to talk about that."

"Maybe she wasn't into small details like I am. At work I'm the only one who seems to care if the sugar and jelly packets and mustard and ketchup packets are in the right holders."

"That's where my dad hit me. That's where the belt buckle cut me."

"You mean, he hit you with a belt?"

"Probably needed stitches but he sent me to bed. In the morning he beat me again because of the bloody sheets."

"Oh baby. That's horrible," Jackie said, as if she herself was feeling the pain. Karl thought about how Jackie made him feel and about how Claire made him feel, and he decided that for all her rough edges and her temper problem, Claire was the woman he really loved, the woman he had always loved. Good thing his back was turned to Jackie as his tears wet the pillow.

Blanche called her and they arranged to meet at Muggs, where Claire ordered a cappuccino. She noticed that Blanche was more attractive than she had ever seen her. Normally, she didn't bother to do her hair, just let it fall, creating a bedraggled, middle-aged hippie sort of look, but today her hair had sheen and bounce, and she was wearing lipstick and eye shadow.

"You look like you're going on a job interview or something," Claire said.

"No, just wanted to look nice," Blanche said. "Maybe it's my renewed optimism about life in general. I found a guy."

"No, hush, you did not, what's his name?"

"Greer. Jack Greer."

"How'd you meet him?"

"It was the craziest thing, a perfect accident, or maybe pure fate, like something destined to happen, because you could never have dreamed it up or planned it."

"You better tell me," Claire said.

"I was at the Bubblemat, you know, doing a load, and just minding my own business, reading a movie star magazine with pictures of actresses without their makeup, looking like shit ... you know, without their makeup those women look just like you and me, just average and homely as hell ... and that's when Jack walks in, and he's carrying a Subway sandwich bag and wearing coveralls, brown Carhartts with paint on them, and I don't even think he's cute at first because I just see the coveralls and figure he's another drunk house painter. I don't know why it is that painters are always such drinkers, but anyway, when he turns around I can see his face and I'm like 'oh my god he's gorgeous,' and he really is gorgeous. He's got a headful of jet black hair, wavy and just, well, he's just as handsome as Sean Connery or George Clooney, a really rugged kind of handsome. I swear to god he could be an actor, and baby I just stared at him, because even in those coveralls I swear he's getting me hot and bothered. And I thought I had gotten over men, I swear, I thought I was done with them, until he walked in."

Claire could see that the brakes had gone out on Blanche's mouth and just sipped the cappuccino while she blabbed. Not that she wasn't happy for her, she just couldn't find a place to insert a comment.

"So there he is, this god-like creature in dirty coveralls, trying to fix the coin box on one of the dryers, and he turns and looks at me over his shoulder like he could feel my eyes on him ... he told me later that he felt my eyes going up and down his back like fingers at a Vietnamese massage parlor ... and he looks, and he smiles at me, and baby I was over the moon. He didn't know it, but I was. He could have had me right there on the grimy tile floor of the Bubblemat with a whole roomful of chubby Mexican women watching and I would not have cared."

"My god, Blanche," Claire said.

"Yeah I know."

"He's that hot, huh?" Claire asked, like they were in high school talking about guys on the football team.

"He is *that* hot, baby girl," Blanche said emphatically. "*That* hot."

"My god."

"So I think he knows he's tormenting me. He finishes with the coin box and goes and sits down behind the counter like he owns the place, which I find out later he does own the place, so that explains why he acted like it, and he sits there and eats his sandwich and drinks a Pepsi. Turns out he is addicted to Pepsis but he refuses to drink the diet ones, no, he's a sugar consumer and drinks the real thing, and he says its his only guilty pleasure other than sex, and baby it turns out this man is addicted to sex."

"Addicted? I didn't know you could get addicted to it," Claire said.

"Yes, addicted, as in he's gotta have it at least once a day to feel normal. That's how he puts it, and I think it's because his body has become addicted to the endorphins, at least that's what I found out when I Googled it."

"So what happened? I mean, you guys got together? Is it serious?"

"Serious? Hmmm, yeah, I'd say it is, but it's getting to be a lot of exercise, making love all the time, whenever he wants."

"Can't you just say no? I mean, sometimes?"

"I can, but I don't want to. I think I'm getting addicted, too. I've never made love like this to any man. That afternoon, the afternoon I met him, we went to my house and made love in my bedroom. I had never made love in my bedroom in the afternoon, and I didn't realize that the cats like to lounge on my bed in the afternoon because that's when the sun is coming through the windows. And he made me stretch out on the bed and kissed every square inch of my body ... I mean *every* square inch ... and the cats, Tom and Jerry and Pooh Bear, just watched me, half asleep, and stretched out their paws to massage his legs while he was kissing my body and driving me absolutely fuckin' nuts." Claire was impressed, what woman would not be impressed by Jack Greer, laundromat owner and sex-addicted guru of love? She thought about Ryan and how he had made her feel. She thought about sharing a sex story about him but then changed her mind. Then she realized that she was ashamed of what she'd done with Ryan. Even though he had made her feel like a woman, and their lovemaking had really been nothing more than a flesh fix, it had been freeing somehow for her to give in to what her body desired and to go with that and just live in the hormonal land where physical pleasure mattered more than anything else. But that wasn't a place Claire could stay in, that place was not where she felt good about herself. Maybe it was her mother's shame that kept her from enjoying sex the way Blanche did.

"The next day he came by the house again, in the afternoon, and we made love outside in the yard under the muscadine trellis. We got completely naked and screwed our brains out on the ground like two wild animals. My backside was smashing into warm muscadines that had fallen all over the ground and the juice was all over us and it smelled like wine because those muscadines had started to ferment inside their skins. We took a shower together and Jack said my back and my ass looked like he had beaten me with his fists because the muscadines had left purple splotches that looked just like bruises."

Claire was looking at the white ceramic bottom of her mug. It was like a movie screen where she could see Blanche and Jack in their own personal porno flick. She thought about Storm Eagle and what it would be like to make love to a man his size, how he would hold her and position her and what positions they could try and how she would try to please him. Would he like a girl like her, slim and athletic with just a slight pooch from carrying two babies?

"Jack's a millionaire, too," Blanche said. "He owns a chain of sixteen Bubblemats. They're all over North and South Carolina and Virginia. He lives in a big house in Richmond, a big, old, historic house on Regal Hill. Georgian. The kind of place I love. You know I love old, historic houses that smell like Old English Furniture Polish and pipe tobacco. He smokes ten dollar cigars. He drinks single malt scotch called Saint Magdalene that he imports from Ireland. He has a Land Rover and a Mercedes coupe. He's a sailor, too, has his own cutter that he keeps in Virginia Beach. He's taken me sailing. He likes to make love on his boat. I'd never made love on a sailboat before, but when the water's smooth and the wind is nice you can just put the boat on automatic and make love on cushions in the bow, let the sun beat down and rock your bodies to the rhythm of the waves. It's heavenly, Claire. It's like nothing I've ever experienced before. I swear, if I died tomorrow, I could say I've lived well because I've screwed well, and screwed well with a man I love. Whether or not he loves me, or loves me the way I love him, that's another matter."

"You don't know? Sounds like he loves you," Claire said.

"I know he loves to make move to me, I know that much," Blanche said. "I guess a girl can't complain when she gets that much from a guy who's as cute as Jack Greer."

Tyler steered the pontoon boat with conviction, as if imagining himself aboard the Pequod. He had brought the class to White Lake, a gigantic bowl created by a meteorite, filled with crystal clear spring water.

"After it burned through the atmosphere, the meteor that made this lake was probably no bigger than a VW bus. Imagine how fast it had to be going when it plummeted to earth, imagine the explosion that made this hole, it had to be bigger than a nuclear bomb."

"Why are we here?" Hector asked.

"I want each of you to write a poem about the lake. We'll read them tomorrow in class," Tyler explained. Tyler had been coming to the lake by himself to work on his second novel. It represented escape from the lifelessness of manmade structures and the pettiness of academia, a place where he could emerse himself in his story universe. He had wanted to see it again before heading to Barstow.

They docked the pontoon at the far side of the lake, near an area with restaurants and a small amusement park. The amusements had not yet opened for the evening, but you could hear the faint laughter of children lingering in the air from the night before. A few park employees were arriving for the evening shift. They all wore matching orange shirts. A popcorn vendor was popping a fresh batch of popcorn in his popping machine on the sidewalk, sending up a stream of steam. A fudge shop was open and they went inside and watched a woman pour a huge potful onto a marble slab, smoothing out the velvety chocolate to chill. Claire was standing beside Hector. He seemed intrigued by the fudge-making process. He was normally quiet but he would talk to Claire. Claire could tell by the soccer jerseys Hector wore every day that he loved Mexico. He was the son of illegal immigrants who came to Samson County for the peach harvest in 1990 and never left.

"Let's get some fudge," Claire said. "I'll split some with you." She knew Hector didn't have much money, but neither did she. Her spending money was what she earned working at Blueberry Knoll on weekends. She still owed Marla for SCC tuition, and the medical bills would probably make her and Karl go bankrupt.

She knew from his poetry that Hector's father was an alcoholic, so she figured his situation was just as bad. Most everybody in the class had serious financial, mental, psychological or emotional limitations, but that didn't stop them from writing poems. Tyler had taught them that art is forged under stress and that working within your boundaries gave you discipline. She and Hector split a quarter pound of peanut butter fudge.

Behind them the lake shone like a plate of diamonds as the class stood shoulder to shoulder and the popcorn vendor snapped a picture with Tyler's camera. The intense backlight left their faces in the dark. When he put the photo on Facebook he would have to identify each of them by their silhouette, but he would know Claire by the bright red flames of hair suspended in the wind.

As they boarded the pontoon boat for the return ride, Tyler stepped close to her and said, "Your poems are a lot like this lake, Claire, you see straight to the bottom of things." Claire wasn't sure what he meant. She would think about it a thousand times in the years to come. She knew it was a compliment by the way he had said it, and the look in his eyes had conveyed more than he put into words. His eyes said *"I believe in you."*

She looked through the bottom of the boat at the shimmering fish bunched in their school, swimming in unison, following close to the hull, hoping for a morsel of fudge or popcorn. She thought about the poem she would write about this day.

The old chieftain, Shining Owl, was sweeping the linseed-stained floor of the Croatan Lodge with a yellow straw broom. He stopped when he saw Claire's feet in the aisle.

"Can you stuff a wolf pup?" Claire asked. "I noticed you don't have one on display anywhere."

"Storm Eagle can stuff anything. Did you kill it?"

"No, my brother did."

"I thought maybe you ran over it. Where is it?"

"It's in a freezer at his garage. I'll go get it. Should I bring it here?"

"No, take it to the workshop. Go down the road a quarter mile, you'll see a red mailbox. The driveway is long but there's a house at the end. The workshop is behind the house."

Claire drove to McGill's Gulf.

"What are you doin'?" Jeb asked when he saw her duck into the office.

"I'm gettin' your wolf pup stuffed," Claire yelled.

"Where are you takin' it?"

"To Storm Eagle."

"He's a damn good skinner," Jeb said. He stood in the office doorway wiping motor oil from his fingers with a red rag. "I'm glad you're paying for it," Jeb said, "stuffin' ain't cheap." Claire held the wolf pup in both arms. The way its legs stuck out it looked like a small statue wrapped in plastic.

"I'm not paying for it. I'm giving it to him." She brushed past Jeb.

"What? I shot that pup myself."

"I won't mention it to Storm Eagle. He might wanna skin you."

She drove down the long uneven driveway until she came to a small house. She got out, picked up the pup from where it lay on the passenger seat and walked around back calling Storm Eagle's name. He came to the door of his taxidermy shed.

"Grandfather said you were coming. Let's have a look at this little fellow," Storm Eagle said. He was smiling. It was the first time she'd seen his teeth. He had a handsome smile that make her smile.

"Too bad about that wolf pup, dyin' so young," Claire said.

"Something this wild doesn't deserve to be frozen, does it. Something this beautiful deserves to run with its brothers. Look at him, those little pink pads, and he's got a perfect black nose. This little fella runs with the great pack now." Storm Eagle had laid the wolf on a wooden table that was stained with animal blood. Claire figured it was where he did the skinning. There were several sharp knives in a wooden tray. Storm Eagle picked up a knife that fit snugly in his hand. It had a razor-sharp curved blade. He made an incision in the wolf pup's belly and proceeded to disembowel it. He plopped the guts into a blue enamel basin.

"How'd you learn about this?" Claire asked.

"What? How to mount animals?"

"Yeah."

"From my grandfather. Some of my people say it is a sacrilege. They say the body and soul must rest together. I say the soul never rests, and the body returns to earth. See how the skin peels back from the frozen muscle? The skin I'll preserve, the body I'll bury."

"How long before you bury it?"

"Thirty minutes maybe."

"Where?"

"Out back."

"I'll wait."

"Why?" He looked at her. He was curious.

"I want to say a prayer over him," she said. Storm Eagle grinned.

Inside the skinning shed, Claire sat on a stool and watched Storm Eagle work. After he slid the skin off the body and up the neck using the small palm knife, he used shears to snip the paws from the legs and a huge Bowie knife to sever the head just below the jaw. He wrapped the carcass in sheets of Tribal Times and carried it behind the shed. He handed Claire a shovel and they walked into the woods.

The sun was a half hour above the horizon, and the light was powerful enough to sieve through the tall scrub pines, turning the forest floor into a golden carpet of needles.

"Let's find a place with an opening to the sky," Storm Eagle said. They found a spot and Claire started digging. Storm Eagle pried the shovel from her hands. His weight pushed the shovel deep and in two minutes he'd created a good hole. Claire placed the pup in it.

"You go first," he said. It took a second for Claire to realize what he was talking about.

"Sure," she said and bowed her head. Storm Eagle looked heavenward. "Dear God," Claire prayed, "this pup didn't do anything wrong. Jeb just shot him kind of by accident. Please let him into heaven. Please look after him."

"Oh Great Spirit," Storm Eagle prayed, "take this little one into the land without pain, without hunger, where he can run with the bobcats and black bears."

Night was coming on, a few stars at a time. After washing up, they drove to The Inferno for cold beers. Storm Eagle even let her talk him into a game of pool.

"Why did you come by today?" Storm Eagle asked, looking up from his cue stick. "Don't say it was about the wolf pup."

"I can't explain it."

"Okay. Don't try," he said. "I'm glad you did."

After she beat him at pool, Claire drove Storm Eagle back to his house. She'd never known a man like him, and she wanted to tell him so, and something in her longed for him to hold her. He had dated white girls before and liked them for the most part. He walked around the car and opened her door without saying anything. She looked up at him wondering what he might do. She saw in his eyes what he wanted to do. He cupped her head in his hand and bent over to kiss her. He knew she wanted him to kiss her. Indians can sense such things. His mouth tasted lightly of tobacco and nutmeg, tinged with peppermint and Pabst.

Then he seemed to lift her effortlessly out of the car and

into his arms. He kissed her again. His arms and hands were so large and strong she felt like she was being held by a grizzly bear or pro football player.

"Do you want to come in?" he asked. Claire ran it all through her mind, and just about every ounce of her wanted to make love to the huge, wise, smooth-skinned Indian, but there was one ounce of her that knew better.

As she was leaving, an '86 Chevy Impala was parked at an angle in Storm Eagle's long driveway, blocking her turn onto the gravel road that would take her to the blacktop. She stopped the Wrangler about twenty feet away from the Impala and was studying the situation when two people got out and began walking toward her. She threw the Jeep into reverse but before she stepped on the gas someone had jumped into the seat beside her: a white man, short and stocky, with thick, stubby hands like Visegrips. He must have come up behind her. He grabbed the steering wheel just as the Jeep jumped backward and slammed into a Loblolly Pine. She could hear needles falling on the Wrangler's canvas roof softly like light rain.

The other two men appeared as dark shapes approaching in her headlights. One of them stood in the gravel lane to keep watch, the other walked to her side of the Jeep. She had never seen the men before. The man who spoke to her had a shaved head and looked like he lifted weights. He wore camper shorts and an orange tanktop with a Clemson logo.

"Hey, what's up, Claire? That's your name, right?"

"What do you want?" she asked through tight, angry lips. She felt a wild fury building within her.

"You probably think we want to rape you, huh? Well,

194

this is your lucky night. We just came to bring a message." He reached over and pushed the hair away from her left ear. "Listen up, little girl, this is important. You know the big brick house over at the country club? You know that house?"

"Yeah, I know it."

"Well, I 'spect you do. Don't go near that house again. Understand? Never ever again. Or you will be raped. Raped by all three of us. And a lot worse." He reached forward. She thought he was going to touch her breasts because his hand was moving toward her chest when something came flying out of the woods and hit the bald man in the side of the head, like a bat hitting a baseball. He crumpled to the ground. Then Claire saw a figure in her peripheral vision, but it was not until the figure was illuminated by the headlights that she recognized Storm Eagle. He must have run all the way from his house, a good half-mile. The other two were squaring off against him, one had pulled a knife, Storm Eagle held a Louisville Slugger, swung it slowly in front of him, back and forth. It looked small in his hand.

"Come on, try me," he said calmly. The bald guy on the ground came to in pain, moaning, only half-concious. The one without a knife ran for the car, the other man followed. They jumped in and locked the doors. Either the Impala refused to start or they had lost the key, or maybe the bald guy had the key. The men covered their faces as Storm Eagle smashed the windshield.

Claire got out of the Jeep and hunted for the bald guy's wallet. In it he carried a Blockbuster card and driver's license. By the light of the headlamps she could read his name: Wallace Jackson.

Storm Eagle jumped on the hood of the Impala and smashed the windshield until it was a sheet of glistening shards, then he stomped on it with the heel of his boot. The man on the driver's side of the car jumped out and ran. Storm Eagle jumped off the car and pulled the other man across the front seat like a rag doll, then threw him onto the ground. He kicked him several times hard enough to roll the guy over in the brutal gravel, then he sat on him and twisted the man's arm behind his back. Claire thought he was going to snap it off like a chicken wing, the way it was cocked back.

"Storm Eagle, stop! Don't kill him," Claire yelled. Storm Eagle paused. He looked at the arm he had in his grip. Then he let out a bloodcurdling scream, like an Indian warrior celebrating a kill, or on the verge of killing: he seized a fistful of the man's hair and began slamming his face into the road, making a bloody pulp of his nose and lips. Claire rushed over and sprang onto Storm Eagle's shoulders, riding him like a wild horse she was trying to tame. He had enough presence of mind to know he could hurt her if he didn't gain control of himself, because she was determined to keep him from killing the man and clung to his neck until he stopped.

He wrapped his huge arms around her small body, and it was only then that she realized he was weeping.

In a half hour, Sheriff Clancy showed up, and right behind him the EMTs. The two men were tied to the bumper of the Impala.

"Who wants to explain what happened here?" The Sheriff asked.

"Those men blocked the driveway," Claire said. "Then

196

they threatened me."

"But they didn't harm you?"

"No, but they said they were going to rape me. That's when Storm Eagle got here."

"Where were you?" the Sheriff asked, scrutinizing the Indian's face.

"Claire dropped me off at my house. I ran down here."

"How did you know she was in trouble?"

"I watched her drive away. I saw her tail lights and saw the Jeep back into the woods. So I started running."

"You fucked them boys up pretty bad."

"That one there" – Storm Eagle pointed to the one whose face he had smashed into the road – "he killed my brother."

Storm Eagle, Claire and the Sheriff drove to the convenience store where Little Wolf had been shot and killed. Storm Eagle had a key because the store belonged to him and his grandfather. He turned on the lights.

"This is where my brother was lying, there behind the counter. Do you remember?"

"I remember very well, Storm Eagle," the Sheriff said. Storm Eagle knelt down close to the floor and touched a spot on a 4x4 post.

"He was lying here, where they left him to die. But before he died he scratched something in this post. Do you see that?" The Sheriff bent over until he could see what was scratched there.

"It looks like a symbol of some kind," the Sheriff said.

"It's the letter A in a circle, the symbol for anarchy," Storm Eagle said, "it's the same symbol that man has on his forearm."

"No shit."

"You can see it for yourself, Sheriff."

"That's a bit of a stretch, isn't it? There's probably a lot of tattoos like that. You almost killed him for that?"

"He's the one. I should have killed him for what he did to my brother."

"Can't you investigate, Sheriff?" Claire asked.

"Oh, I'll surely investigate," the Sheriff said. "Count on it. I'll get to the bottom of this, I surely will."

Awake

By the end of the semester, Claire began to feel like she was being born a third time. This time she wasn't opening inwardly to an awareness of who she was as a spiritual being, she was opening herself to the outer world, she was seeing everything anew through the eyes of a poet.

It was because of Tyler. He had taught her a love of words and poetry. So when Aisha told her that Tyler was leaving SCC, Claire's immediate reaction was to start crying. Her crying triggered Aisha's emotions and they walked across campus to the parking lot experiencing their own very short but intense trail of tears.

"Why does he have to leave?" Claire asked.

"He's got another job. He's going to Barstow."

"What's that?"

"It's a college up in the Blue Ridge Mountains. But it's not a typical college. It's a commune, very organic, where the students do all the farming. It's mostly artists. They have a great creative writing program."

"Is it expensive to go there?"

"It's not cheap," Aisha said, opening the door to her Forester, "but there's always student loans."

"We'll be sisters for real if you say yes," Claire said, sitting across from Marla at Applebees. Jeb had asked Marla to marry him and she was dancing on the decision precipice.

"I think maybe I've always loved him. In high school I thought so. We dated for almost three years."

"Do you like his company? They say you've got to be best friends first and lovers second."

"Who say's that?"

"I read it somewhere."

"You know Jeb. He's funny sometimes the way he acts all pissed off but then sometimes he'll crack me up."

"Sounds like most men," Claire said. "If you want I can get you a deal on Blanche's marriage factory."

"That'd be super. We don't want to spend a whole lot. I can't believe I'm even considering this."

"It's not like you have to rush into anything, Marla. Unless you're pregnant or something." Claire wasn't about to mention Cherry.

"Pregnant? Hell no. I just don't want to make the same mistake twice."

"The same mistake? You think it was a mistake to dump him before? He was two-timin' you."

"He'd never do that again. He knows I'd kill him," Marla said.

"Oh really," Claire rolled her eyes, "well, if it happens, killing won't do any good, because the love will be ruined, spoiled, like a gallon of milk gone sour. That's a metaphor."

"Yes it is," Marla said.

A week later, Claire got a call from Myrtle Beach. "We

did it," Marla said. "We did it. I'm wearing a gigantic zirconium ring from the Gay Dolphin."

"That's great, Marla. I'll tell Blanche the big wedding is off." Claire hung up the phone. She had a new sister-in-law. She'd always wanted a sister. She walked into the den and looked at her boys watching TV and wondered what they would grow up to become. Would they be smart? How could they expect to be anything more than what she and Karl were? She heard the door latch click. Speak of the devil. It was Karl. The boys ran to him to see if he had brought them anything from Walmart. When they discovered he was giftless they returned to the sofa.

"Are you staying for dinner?" Toby asked.

"I don't know. If your mother will let me, maybe," he said. Claire got another frozen hamburger out of the freezer. She popped open a beer for herself and handed Karl a Coke. He still had a bandage on his nose from when Howie had broken it.

"What do you want? What are you here for?" Claire asked.

"I just wanted to see you."

"You been havin' second thoughts? You realizin' what you said goodbye to? What a catch I really am?"

"Something like that, I guess."

"Well, it's too late for second chances," Claire said. Karl turned to face her while she shook seasoning on the burger patties.

"I talked to the district super about getting some insurance. Turns out I'll need a 'supplemental policy,' so they'll be taking that out of my paycheck now to cover the boys and you. First time I ever heard of a supplemental. They ought to tell you that shit when they hire you."

"I doubt they'll cover Sam, since he has a pre-existing condition."

"I don't suppose they will," Karl said, "but I'll ask." It only made sense that they would have to pay over a quarter million dollars to the hospital. That was par for the fuckin' course as Big Eddie liked to say.

"You said something to me once, when we were havin' one of our knock down drag outs," Karl said.

"What was that?"

"You said I would never amount to anything more than a drunk. Like my father. That's what you said."

"I'm sorry I said that, specially since he's dead and all now. I know that must've hurt. But you were hurting me at the time."

"I know. It was probably the beer talkin'. You got any pot?"

"I quit."

"Really? That's good, Claire. That's great. You want me to go look for some tomatoes?" Karl slipped out the back door. The tomato plants were still profuse with red fruit, some ripe ones split open with weepy slits, a few rotted ones. Karl tossed the rotted ones toward the hand-built deer stand he'd never put to use. Maybe he'd put it to use. Hell yes, maybe he'd drop a six pointer. That would show Claire. He balanced three ripe tomatoes in one hand.

Inside he sliced them onto a plate, pretty as a picture.

They sat together as a family again. He told them some funny stories he'd heard from his buddies at work.

He reminded himself that he and Claire were still legal, all they'd done was separate. But the thought held no comfort. He could sense in her a dislike for him and a distance between them, a distance created by hundreds of nights of drinking and fighting. Too bad when you grow up too late to salvage what's best about your life.

Tyler's going away party got a little crazy. He danced with his female students, and everybody was drunk on Purple Jesus. Some of the girls danced raunchy, especially Aisha, but then she was in love with him, or his writing, and had already made plans to transfer to Barstow. Ryan wasn't there, and Claire was glad. She danced with Hector and danced one time with Tyler. He held her hands and spun her around. She could see he was having a great time. Later he sat beside her on the sofa and put his arm around her shoulders. He told her she was a naive poet, like the naive artists who lived somewhere in West Virginia or Kentucky who painted pictures on pieces of old plywood and barn siding and he'd even seen one who painted on a piece of aluminum torn off a mobile home. That one painted with an artificial hand because it had been blown off in Korea and the other had arthritis. Naive didn't mean she was stupid, he reassured her. And besides, you don't have to be smart to be a good poet, he said, you just have to be able to bend language to your will. Then, without a word of warning, he leaned over and kissed her on the cheek, but his lips brushed her ear and made her blush, her whole body went hot, and she would have kissed him on the mouth if he'd wanted her to. She realized she loved him, but not exactly in a normal way. More like the way you love someone you can never have, an infatuation best left dormant, a romance best left to the imagination.

She was on the way home when the Sheriff pulled up behind her, his blue lights pulsing in her rearview.

"Can I buy you a cup of coffee?" he asked when he got to her window.

They sat at the counter inside the 24-Hour Diner. Jackie Mackie walked over and took their order totally pretending she didn't know who Claire was. Claire looked at her in her tangerine waitress blouse and skin-tight black jeans. She looked cute. No wonder Karl was attracted to her. When Jackie brought them coffee, she stole a glance at Claire. She knew Claire was prettier than her, and skinnier, and fiesty. Just the kind of girl who was hard to keep down. Neither of them felt enough hatred or spite to break their silence.

Sheriff Clancy slurped his coffee, then his eyes angled up and locked on Claire's face. "When I saw the mess out there at Storm Eagle's my first suspicion was that your husband was behind it, you know, after he got that beating, maybe he wanted pay back."

"You knew about him getting beat up?"

"Word gets around, Claire." His eyes narrowed. "But I don't guess you know anything about that?"

"Not a thing."

"Alright. Well. That fella with the tattoo finally confessed. So I guess we have you to thank, you and Storm Eagle, for a murder solved."

"Storm Eagle, not me."

"We also found out who hired those men to threaten you. It was Helen Dorsey. If they agree to testify against her, she may go to prison."

"She won't survive long in there, sick as she is."

"Be that as it may, I have to bring charges. Claire, there's something else I need to ask you. Storm Eagle told me his side of the story, how you brought him the wolf, then you and him went to The Inferno, then you took him home. But why'd you go see him in the first place?"

"I just wanted to give him the wolf pup," Claire said.

"But why? What motivated you to do that?" The Sheriff was rubbing his chin. Claire thought he had probably been a handsome young man but now he was at least sixty, and he looked worn down, grizzled, hardened by life.

"I really don't know. It was just something I wanted to do. That wolf pup had been in the freezer. I thought Storm Eagle would appreciate it. I asked him to stuff it." The way the Sheriff looked at her she could tell he didn't believe her. He was probably thinking she was a loose woman and wanted to sleep with Storm Eagle. That was true, but she had to let him wonder, because she was wondering herself what it would be like to fall in love with a man like Storm Eagle and why she didn't stay that night when she had the chance.

The meth lab where Cherry got her face scarred had been run by a friend of Johnny C's named Cooter Winstead. Cooter had not been there when the lab exploded, he was at home asleep. Cherry had wandered by, not looking to buy meth, but simply looking for Cooter because he'd promised to loan her some money she needed to fix her car. Since she had broken up with Jeb, he wouldn't fix her old Sunbird for free and it needed a radiator.

The Sunbird had been parked at the garage where Jeb could see it everyday while Cherry was in the psychiatric hospital. He went ahead and put a radiator in it at his own expense. When she came to see him after she got out, he'd even washed it and waxed it and parked it at an angle in front of the garage. He'd just gotten back from Myrtle Beach and his new gold band still had its sheen.

"Thank you, Jeb," Cherry said, her hand aimlessly stroking the hood of the Sunbird. The breeze carried the tobacco-like scent of Autumn leaves, and it caught her hair, flipping a strand into her mouth.

"No biggie," he said. He had trouble looking at her without staring at the pink scars on her right cheek and forehead. It was like she had turned away the second of the explosion.

"The key's inside. I'll get it," Jeb said. Cherry followed him into the garage. As he was reaching for the key hanging in the wooden key box, he felt her hands slide around his stomach, her breasts pressing into the small of his back, her head resting between his shoulder blades.

"I've missed you," she said, and he could feel her warm breath through his baby blue Dickey. He didn't know how to answer. A gas customer drove up and he wiggled out of her arms to pump the gas and squeegee the windshield. Maybe a minute had passed before he heard the Sunbird crank. It blew out a trail of exhaust – he'd told her the rings were shot to hell – and she disappeared down the highway without looking back.

Claire got the call about 7:00 Tuesday night. Grams had been rolled down the hall to the palliative care room, where the entire family could sit with her. Her body had already drawn up like a corn husk, now they were waiting for her lungs and heart to quit. Her two most vital organs were still doing their jobs, and her brain was sending signals, but she couldn't open her eyes. She hadn't eaten or taken water in three days.

J.J. and Big Eddie were already there. Jeb and Marla had arrived about 9:00. Big Eddie had walked down to the cafeteria to get a sandwich before they closed.

"Where are the boys?" J.J. asked when Claire arrived.

"I took them to Blanche's. Do you think I should have brought them to say goodbye?"

"No, they'd've been scared to death." J.J. didn't look up from her needlepoint.

"Why are you doing needlepoint? You never do needlepoint," Claire said.

"I know how stubborn that old woman is. This could take a couple of days. Oh Lord," J.J. muttered. Karl had walked in. Claire had never seen his hair so neat, he was clean-shaven, and his cologne wafted ahead of him. He surveyed the room quickly and shook Jeb's hand, gave Marla a friendly hug, then turned toward Claire and J.J.

"Hi Claire, J.J. Good to see you. Sorry for the circumstances. How is Grams?"

"She's hangin' on," Claire said. "No telling when she'll let go."

"Is she conscious?" Karl asked.

"She hasn't been conscious for over a year," J.J. said. "Not in the sense of knowing who she is or who anybody else is, or where she is, or what day it is, or anything else, God bless her."

"How are you, Claire?" Karl asked in a soft tone.

"I'm good," Claire said. "I think I'll go look for Daddy before he gets himself in trouble. I could use some coffee."

"When did you start drinking coffee?" J.J. asked.

"When I discovered cappucinos," Claire said.

When Claire had left the room, J.J. looked at Karl with narrowed, threatening eyes.

"You better take care of her and them boys of yours."

"I'm tryin' to, J.J. I even asked her back, but she wouldn't have none of that. Honestly though, I can't blame her."

"You've got responsibilities, don't forget that."

"Don't you think I know that," Karl said.

Claire found Big Eddie in the darkened cafeteria.

"Hey peanut," he said when she walked in.

"Hey Daddy."

"You need some coffee? There's a machine." He stretched into his pocket and got out a handful of quarters that spun and sang on the formica table. Claire picked up four quarters and walked to the machine. She decided to get a French Vanilla. The falling of the coins echoed through the empty cafeteria. Claire sat with her father and sipped the hot creamy liquid. He was looking at the hands cradling his cup of coffee as if they weren't his own. She knew he didn't like things like this, that it took a lot out of him.

"Why do you suppose I'm the first person in the family to ever go to college?" Claire asked.

"You always were a smart girl. When you were little you used to count your toes over and over."

"Grams was smart. She liked to read," Claire said. She'd been thinking about why it was that her grandmother had never stepped foot outside Sampson County except for two trips to the ocean, one when she was a girl and one when she was sixty-five. How was it possible for her to be happy in a life like that?

"She made the best cabbage and corn beef you ever tasted," Big Eddie said.

"I remember it," Claire said.

"She was a tough old Irish broad," Big Eddie said. "Just like you."

"I'm not old. Not yet."

"You know what I mean."

"I'm gonna go back up. I haven't even said goodbye to her yet."

"You go on. I'll be up in a while," Big Eddie said.

Claire held her grandmother's hand. There was very little warmth in it, no strength.

"Well Grams," she half-whispered. "I guess this is goodbye for now. You were a good grandma. Thanks for teaching me to play the piano and always having neopolitan around when I came for a sleepover, and everything else you did for me."

Around ten, Pastor Owens arrived. He looked tired but his smile and confidence made everyone feel better.

"I mean, this is a handsome family, isn't it. What a shame you have to go through this, but it is a natural process, isn't it, I mean, and it's good you can be here for Mrs. McGill." He walked over to the bedside and prayed over Grams. Then he sat down beside Claire.

"I hope she goes to be with Jesus," Claire said.

"You should have told me she was here. I would have dropped in to see her. We could have made sure of her salvation."

"You mean you would have driven over to see her?" Claire asked. The nursing home was an hour drive from Newton Grove.

"I spend half my life driving to see people. The Lord rides with me, though, and we have some good talks."

Karl had gotten very quiet when the pastor arrived. He had been caught in sin with Jackie but had yet to fess up to it and correct his backslidden condition, but he knew the time would come when he would have to get right with Jesus again, he knew it and Pastor Owens knew it, too.

"Have you made arrangements for the funeral?" Pastor Owens asked Claire.

"I don't know. Momma, have we made funeral arrangements?"

"Your grandmother is not dead yet, Claire."

"I know that, Momma, the pastor was just asking, for goshsake."

"No, we have not made arrangements, but I know she

wanted a white casket with gold handles. She told me so several times."

"Well, when the time comes, let me know and I'll be glad to help," Pastor Owens said. "I'll be glad to do the service." Claire squeezed his arm and rested her head on his shoulder.

"I'm glad you're here," she said.

Marla and Jeb stood beside Grams. Jeb was so tore up he couldn't talk. Marla stroked his arm. Big Eddie walked in. He seemed upset.

"Did you hear that banshee?" he asked.

"No, we didn't hear anything, Daddy," Claire said.

"I was walking down the hallway and I'd swear I heard a banshee screaming its fool head off."

"What's a banshee?" Marla asked.

"A banshee is what you hear before death comes, the banshee screaming," Big Eddie said.

"That's just an old Irish superstition," Jeb said.

"It was probably somebody in the emergency room getting stitches," Marla said.

"Or having a baby in the birthing room," J.J. said. Big Eddie walked over to his mother's bedside. He suspended his hand over her mouth to feel the intensity of her breathing. "She's still with us," he said.

The pastor stepped to the bedside, said another prayer, then excused himself.

Around twelve, Tommy showed up. He'd been drinking. The smell of beer was on him as heavy as Big Eddie's Old Spice.

"Oh my God," he said, "look at her." He walked to

the foot of Grams' bed. "She doesn't look so good." Claire pulled him down into a chair.

"Why did you come over here? You're drunk."

"I heard about Grams and I wanted to be with you," Tommy said. "This is a hard time. Let me be here with you." Tommy draped his arm around her neck. "Oh, hey Jeb. Hey Marla. The happy married couple." Tommy put his hand on Claire's knee, which she promptly removed.

"Stop it, you're drunk, it's embarrassing," she whispered forcefully into his ear. Tommy grinned and turned to Jeb.

"Jeb, you know that baby wolf you killed? It came by Claire's place this afternoon. It had an Indian with it." He looked at Claire. "That Indian asked for you. He wanted to show you the baby wolf he'd stuffed. He did a damn good job. It was lifelike as hell. That damn Indian must have been seven feet tall."

"His name's Storm Eagle," Claire said.

"What were you doing at the trailer?" Karl asked Tommy.

"I was just there, Karl, don't you worry about it."

Karl stood up, stepped toward Tommy. "I should break your face," Karl said, fists balled up tight and white-knuckled.

"Don't worry about me, Karl. I done asked her to marry me and she said no thanks. No thank you, Tommy. I'm not gonna marry another loser ... that's what she was thinking. I'm gonna keep workin' on her, though. If she was to say yes, I'd be your brother-in-law, Jeb. And Karl, I'd be your husband-in-law I guess."

"Come on," Claire said, pulling Tommy to his feet. "Let's get some coffee in you." As they were moving toward the door, Grams made a groaning noise that came from somewhere deep within, maybe the place where her soul had been pried loose. She sighed, her last breath escaping into the room's fluorescent air. They looked at each other and they all knew she had passed over. It was time to talk about the funeral.

Claire awoke to the whine of the air conditioner, which was freezing up. She turned it off and the room was suddenly quiet as a tomb. Sam and Toby were on either side of her. For a good five minutes, she studied Sam's sweet face in the bright sunlight, the nicks and scratches, misquito bites, and soft plasticity of his ears.

She made them waffles with fresh strawberries and slices of banana. She dressed them and dropped them at Jackie's, where Karl was staying. He and Big Eddie were planning to take the boys fishing on Lake Haskings in their new johnboat.

The sun had climbed to its mid-point in the sky when she drove to the dam and parked and walked along it, looking at the smooth lake on one side and the sheer drop on the other. She thought about school and poetry, her boys, Karl, and Storm Eagle. She thought about her Grams and what heaven must be like. Then she thought about herself and what she wanted out of life, and she realized how alone she was. She felt transparent, weightless, more like a thought than a real person, like the way Aisha had described herself that night in the tent.

She climbed onto the low, concrete wall that prevents cars from falling into the valley. She stood there and thought about jumping. She felt utterly inconsequential. Not hopeless, but as helpless as a lost child, and she wondered why the dark thoughts within her welled up the way they did.

The September sky was bluer than any blue she'd ever seen. As a breeze enveloped her, her eyes began to brim with tears. The gust suddenly intensified, nudged her backward, and her feet inched closer to oblivion.

The V of the valley grew darker in the distance, almost black, a cave-like hole between green hills. A barred owl dipped into the valley above the churning water at the spillway, coming upward, toward her, then bent its path, and, for a split second, she thought it was watching her, before it sailed away into the valley's shadowy crease, and she wondered what would become of her life, then for some strange reason she thought of the children who came running to Jesus to sit as his feet and wondered what it would be like to lean against his knee and feel his hand stroke her hair.

She opened her shirt like the owl had opened its broad wings, letting the wind billow inside it like a kite, letting the fairy on her breast catch a few rays while the sun warmed her lips and eyelids. A smile took control of her mouth, a feeling of wholeness approaching joy rose within her, then she was laughing for no reason at all, feeling more alive than ever before. Alive, and wide awake.

Dear Reader of My Poetry:

When Professor Tyler told us in his class we had to write a poem about sometime when we touched God's face, this is the poem I wrote. It's called "Faces" and it's about my boy Sam and all the children of the world and all the mommas.

Claire McGill

PS. I don't know what grade I might have gotten. I never turned it in to get it graded so I am sending it to the professor one day soon. He has moved to a hippie college called Barstow to teach more creative writing in the foothills of North Carolina which is my home state and not that far a drive if I ever wanted to visit there.

Faces

When I touch
Sam's sweet face
and roundness of eyes
under lids and eyelashes
silky perfect him sleeping
like that and breathing
real soft like he's on a cloud
floating and when I look up
I see the mobile Daddy
gave us when he was a baby
in his crib with butterflies twirling
around and around in the air
from the air conditioner
and my shoulder is cold
now and my ear and Sam's
ear too and I kiss it
and my lips warm it some
and it reminds me
of a big beautiful wad
of pink BubbleYum
or creek clay smoothed
into a shell shape by God's finger
but he's asleep, he don't know it's me
looking down at his sweetness
and know all my love how deep
it goes down inside of me for him.
And I think about all the faces
on all the children of the world
and all the mommas touching them
like its beauty can be all theirs
or is, cause remember their wombs
and touching them real softly sleeping
they know God his own self gave them
what's worth loving most, some person
other than their own dumb self who
only wants to be cuddled and kissed
and loves them, no questions asked
just like they are, scars and all.

Also by Les Butchart:

- novels -

Sons of Noah
Elyana

- poetry & short stories -

Home Movie

- metaphysics -

The Theory of Everything & Beyond

- motion pictures -

Lake of Fire
The Hive

On the web:

www.lesbutchart.website

- check out my other books, movies & blog -

About the Author

John Leslie Butchart attended the University of North Carolina at Chapel Hill where he studied psychology, philosophy, creative writing and filmmaking.

He and his wife Susan own and operate a digital media company, Artisan Media Group, in Greensboro, North Carolina.

John is also the founder of Highway 29 Motion Pictures, and MoviesAmongFriends.com, a social network for filmmakers and actors.

Author of more than a twenty screenplays, his film credits include *Lake of Fire*, a southern gothic motion picture which he wrote and directed, and *The Hive*, a mystery.

In addition to *The Music We're Born Remembering*, he has authored a book of short stories and poetry entitled *Home Movie;* an apocalyptic thriller, *Sons of Noah;* and an Appalachian romance, *Elyana*.